The Inherited Bride

by

REBECCA STRATTON

Harlequin Books

TORONTO • LONDON • LOS ANGELES • AMSTERDAM
SYDNEY • HAMBURG • PARIS • STOCKHOLM • ATHENS • TOKYO

Original hardcover edition published in 1980
by Mills & Boon Limited

ISBN 0-373-02399-5

Harlequin edition published April 1981

Printed in U.S.A.

"Eduardo, I know she was there...."

Lari was still upset from her ordeal in the elevator. She knew the woman had been there when it had jammed, and she must convince Eduardo. "I saw her standing there..." she began.

"Lari," Eduardo said, "my dear child, who on earth would want to harm you in the way you're implying?"

"I don't know," she said weakly. So many things whirled around in her mind and confused her, and there was nothing she could do.

One thing she *could* do something about, though, was his manner of addressing her. She spoke without hesitation. "And I hope you don't intend making a habit of calling me your child," she told him sharply. "I was under the impression that to get Anchoterrias you were *marrying* me, Eduardo, not adopting me!"

REBECCA STRATTON
is also the author of these
Harlequin Romances

1976—THE GODDESS OF MAVISU
1991—ISLE OF THE GOLDEN DRUM
2006—PROUD STRANGER
2018—CHATEAU D'ARMOR
2036—THE ROAD TO GAFSA
2050—GEMINI CHILD
2078—GIRL IN A WHITE HAT
2091—INHERIT THE SUN
2106—MORE THAN A DREAM
2131—THE SIGN OF THE RAM
2141—THE VELVET GLOVE
2154—DREAM OF WINTER
2173—SPINDRIFT
2180—IMAGE OF LOVE
2201—BARGAIN FOR PARADISE
2222—THE CORSICAN BANDIT
2261—LOST HERITAGE
2268—THE EAGLE OF THE VINCELLA
2274—LARK IN AN ALIEN SKY
2303—CLOSE TO THE HEART
2339—THE TEARS OF VENUS
2356—APOLLO'S DAUGHTER
2376—TRADER'S CAY

and these
Harlequin Presents

106—YELLOW MOON
121—THE WARM WIND OF FARIK

CHAPTER ONE

LARI had been listening to the car approaching for some time, for sound carried on the hot still air above the valley, and she got up to move restlessly across to the window. The big *salón* was cool, but still Lari felt an uncomfortable film of dampness across her forehead and her hands felt sticky as she watched the car's progress along the approach road.

Scarcely worthy of the name road, the route through the vineyards was narrow and rutted by the passage of tractors and lorries until it was nothing more than a rough track. A swirl of white dust marked the car's progress where it rose above the low-growing vines, and as she noted it Lari mused on the fact that Eduardo had sense enough not to race his expensive horse-power over such terrain.

He would remember the state of the road, of course, even though it was six years since he last visited his uncle's estate, and she was trying to imagine what his feelings must be, when a short, dark woman appeared in the doorway. Lari turned swiftly, her senses alert and anxiety shadowing her blue eyes with darkness.

'He's coming, *señorita*!'

The woman's excitement would have been infectious even had she not already been tingling with it herself, and Lari smiled as she moved back across the room, knowing that Marta Sedova noted every betraying sign with her sharp black eyes. 'Yes I've seen him, thank you, Marta. When you've shown Señor Eduardo in, will you bring us some wine, please?'

'Of course, *señorita*. The San José?'

Prepared to trust her judgment as she always did,

Lari nodded. 'Whatever you think best.' She managed a smile and colour touched the paleness of her cheeks. 'I want to impress Señor Eduardo with our best.'

'Of course.' Marta Sedova had spent nearly forty years of her life at Anchoterrias in the service of the Sagrera family, and she had in that time acquired certain privileges not enjoyed by the rest of the staff. Having known her late employer's stepdaughter since Lari was a small girl she had an affection for her that was not always evident in her rather forbidding expression, but she smiled understanding of the tightly clasped hands and shadowed eyes. 'He was always kind to you, little one, do you remember?'

Unable to deny it, Lari managed another faint smile. 'Yes, of course I remember, Marta. But I was a schoolgirl then, and now—well, now things are—will be different.'

'Let us hope so!' Marta murmured, and before Lari could comment, she turned to go, muttering to herself as she crossed the *salón*. 'I will attend to the wine, *señorita*; the San José, eh?'

She didn't wait for confirmation but went out, closing the door behind her and leaving Lari to once more contemplate the meeting that was now imminent. More than eleven years ago she had met Eduardo Sagrera for the very first time, on the day she arrived from England with her mother and her newly acquired stepfather, and she had been ten years old at the time.

The bridegroom's family had gathered to wish good health to the newlyweds. As much out of curiosity as good will, Lari had since realised, and to see for themselves the young Englishwoman who had looks and charm enough to lure a quiet widower to the altar for a second time more than twenty years after the death of his first wife. Eduardo Sagrera had been among the guests at his uncle's reception; a tall dark young man of twenty-two who had treated his new little cousin by marriage with gentle politeness and understanding.

Lari's mother had died all too soon afterwards, trying to give birth to a son, and after her death José Sagrera had turned his grief inward, giving all his love and attention to his young stepdaughter instead. Often Lari thought the Sagreras considered he lavished too much on her, and the family of his younger brother in particular. For until José's remarriage it had seemed certain that Eduardo would inherit the bulk of his uncle's fortune, which included the old family estate.

Yet Eduardo had continued to visit Anchoterrias to see his uncle for some years after his marriage. Until, in fact, José's increasing ill-health and desire for solitude, plus Eduardo's involvement in his own family's wine business, caused the visits to taper off and eventually to cease altogether. Not from lack of affection, but because circumstances combined to make it so.

It was a little over six years since the last visit, and Lari felt it would be like meeting a stranger after so long. It was that fact, plus the conditions of her stepfather's will, that were responsible for her present state of mind. Her memory of soft green English fields was very hazy, and she could not now imagine herself living anywhere but in the hot and sometimes harsh Andalusian countryside. It was because she had become so Spanish and he was concerned for her future that José had made what his family doubtless considered a very controversial will, but at the moment Lari wished he had not made it.

'He's here, *señorita*!' Marta appeared briefly again in the doorway without even noticing Lari's nod of acknowledgment or the swift nervous flick of her tongue across dry lips.

The last time Eduardo saw her she had been a child just emerging into womanhood, and already showing promise of the looks that, in her mother, had tempted José Sagrera into a second marriage. The thin young body had now rounded and softened, and the face had become perfectly heart-shaped and delicately pretty, framed in shoulder-length fair hair. Her deep blue eyes at present had a wary look between their thick brown lashes and she again moistened her lips anxiously.

She heard the car stop and the door slam, and brushed her hands down the pale blue dress she wore, wondering suddenly if Eduardo would expect her to be wearing heavy black mourning still. It seemed like an eternity until two lots of footsteps came clicking smartly across the tiled hall floor, then she heard the purring resonance of a deep masculine voice that was quite astonishingly familiar after six years and her heart began to thud hard and fast.

When she realised that Marta's lighter tread was in retreat, Marta apparently having been dismissed, panic soared and fluttered its chill wings in her stomach for a moment, then gave way almost at once to a churning excitement that made her mouth dry and tightened in her throat when at last the *salón* door opened to admit Eduardo Sagrera.

If the intervening years had wrought changes in Lari, they had done the same for Eduardo, but with a more subtle touch. He must be nearly thirty-four now, she realised, and the young man she remembered had become a mature and somewhat severe one; or so it seemed as he stood for a second or two in the doorway, looking at her.

He was always taller than average, and his rangy leanness was stressed by the complimentary cut of a light suit. His dark chiselled features recalled his Moorish ancestry and looked harder and stronger than Lari remembered, black hair and near-black eyes lending strength to the arrogance of his bearing. It was easy to see why he had earned popularity at the local *corridas* as a *torero,* for he had all the necessary qualities required of a bullfighter, even an amateur one.

Lari was thankful that he had never taken it up professionally, for one of the few English idiosyncrasies she retained was a dislike of Spain's national sport. Whether or not he still made occasional appearances at local *fiestas*, she didn't know, and in fact she realised just how little she did know about him. Six years was a long time.

The firm mouth relaxed into a smile as he came across the room to her, and somehow Lari managed to force her unsteady legs into action and moved to meet him. 'Lari!' He leaned and kissed her lightly on both cheeks, and some uncontrollable response in her leapt to welcome it, brief as it was. Straightening up, he took stock of her with bold dark eyes, and the slight thrust of a sensual lower lip was so unexpected that she caught her breath. 'How are you? Fully recovered from the accident?'

'Oh yes, completely, thank you, Eduardo.' Lari tried to suppress the nagging persistence of her conscience that troubled her more than she cared to admit. 'I—I wasn't well enough to go to the funeral, and I wish I could have, but——'

'Ah, no.' Light fingertips touched her cheek for a moment and recalled the gentleness he had once shown to a little English girl in a strange country for the first time, but evoking a much different response in the woman she had since become. 'It was no fault of yours, Lari,' he told her in the voice she remembered so well. 'No one holds you responsible for what happened to Tío José.'

He was cool and reassuring when she had been half afraid he might blame her in some way, and Lari was thankful for it, but she couldn't believe it was an opinion shared by the rest of the Sagrera family. 'No one?' she ventured, and was unaware of the trace of bitterness in her voice.

She was glad he didn't pretend ignorance of her

meaning, for it could only have made his own opinion suspect, and he expressed it without hesitation. '*I* don't hold you responsible in any way at all,' Eduardo insisted, and Lari could well believe that he considered his the only opinion that mattered. Glancing across the room, he indicated two armchairs in a corner near the window. 'Shall we sit down?'

'Oh yes, of course—I'm sorry.'

Eduardo smiled, as if he understood and allowed for her nervousness, seeing her seated before he settled himself into one of the chairs. Leaning back with one leg crossed over the other, he was evidently quite at ease while he regarded her for a moment with an intentness that Lari found infinitely disturbing in the circumstances.

'Has it been very bad for you, Lari?' he asked, and his concern was genuine, she knew. 'How have you been managing? I would have liked to come and do what I could to help, to visit you, but in the circumstances——'

His large expressive hands conveyed his meaning exactly, and it told Lari that one thing at least about Eduardo remained unchanged. The Sagreras still lived by the old standards, and Eduardo as much as the rest of them. It could be that he wished some of the female members of his family had taken it upon themselves to ensure her well-being, but in the event he didn't say so. Instead he let that expressive gesture with his hands say it for him. He had, however, sent flowers for her and she remembered that with gratitude and pleasure.

'Oh, but I understood, of course,' she told him, 'and I was so pleased with the flowers you sent me.'

'Brought you,' he corrected with a faintly rueful smile. 'I thought that at least I could safely come as far as the hospital reception desk!'

Lari recalled how often she would have welcomed

a visitor during the long unhappy days when she was recovering from the accident, but at least he had brought her flowers to the hospital and could still be said to have abided by his family's strict code of morals. In fact it was rather surprising that he had come alone to see her today, and almost as if he followed her train of thought he offered an explanation.

'Strictly speaking I should have brought someone with me on this occasion,' he told her with a faint smile that could in no way be construed as an apology, 'but I preferred to see you alone, Lari; you have no objection, have you?'

The steady dark eyes already knew her answer as they watched her from the shadow of black lashes, and Lari shook her head slowly. 'No, of course I haven't, Eduardo.' She swiftly controlled her wandering thoughts and returned to the original point. 'And I understood why you couldn't see me in hospital, naturally. Your—your family would not have thought it right at all, would they?'

'Would you?' he asked, and the softness of his voice skimmed like an icy finger down her spine.

'It was—hard sometimes.' She spoke slowly, choosing her words and remembering how unutterably lonely and bereft she had felt at that time. It would have helped to see someone, and Eduardo had been so kind and understanding in the old days, yet she couldn't blame him for being influenced by his family, even though he had stepped out of line in this instance. 'I suppose it was with losing Papá like that——'

'Poor little Lari.' His gentleness was something she remembered very well, but his manner was exactly the same as when he had soothed her as a child, and she wondered if he realised that she was now a young woman of twenty-one. 'It must have been hard for you to cope alone, and I'm sorry.'

'Oh, I haven't managed too badly on the whole,' she

assured him, and when she shrugged it was not in any way careless, but because she still found it incredibly hard to mention her stepfather without getting a choking feeling. 'I've been living from day to day and trying to—to forget what happened.'

'That's best.' He offered the comment as consolation, she knew, but it wasn't as easy as he obviously thought.

'I keep thinking that—perhaps if I hadn't been driving so fast I could have——' She shook her head slowly, reliving the familiar nightmare as she had so often done since it happened. 'He loved to go out for a drive sometimes; not very often, just occasionally, and I hadn't the heart to refuse him that day, even though he seemed far from well. He—he slumped against me when he collapsed, you see, and I swerved; I couldn't keep control of the car because of the speed, although I wasn't going so very fast in actual fact. If I hadn't been knocked out myself I might have got help for him and he might have been saved.'

'It was his time, Lari.' The quietly spoken words seemed to give finality to something she had been unable to come to terms with, but yet in some way they were consoling too. 'Did you know what was in his will before Tío José died?'

Lari hadn't expected to be plunged so quickly and so unexpectedly into the situation she had anticipated with such mixed feelings, and for a moment she looked at him uncertainly, finding that dark, intent gaze more disconcerting than ever. 'I—I knew he wanted me to stay on here, he promised me that nothing would change if he could prevent it, and he was anxious that I should stay in Spain.' She smiled faintly when she remembered. 'For some reason Papá liked to think I'd become completely Spanish.'

'And have you?' Without waiting for her to confirm or deny it, Eduardo went on. 'Your Spanish has improved by leaps and bounds since I saw you last; you haven't a trace of accent now.' A glimmer of speculation lurked in the glowing depth of his eyes for a moment and he smiled. 'It's a pity in a way, because that slight accent you had was very attractive.'

Lari accepted the compliment with downcast eyes, for the Eduardo she remembered had never paid those kind of compliments, and he had certainly never looked at her in the bold, speculative way he did now. 'Don't forget that I've been in Spain for over eleven years,' she reminded him, keeping a firm control on her emotions, 'and I've spoken nothing but Spanish since my mother died. Spanish is natural to me now.' She had never felt so ill at ease with him before, and on the spur of the moment she sought relief in normality. 'I asked Marta to bring some wine in when you arrived, but she must have forgotten it. If you'll excuse me a minute, I'll go and see what's happened to it.'

'I told Marta not to disturb us until we rang for her,' Eduardo said, and took note of her blink of surprise. 'We have a great deal to talk about, Lari, and much as I appreciate Marta's devotion, I'd rather we talked privately and without interruption.'

He made no excuse for his having taken the initiative, and Lari recognised it as the first sign of his authority. 'Yes, of course.' She smiled faintly. 'I suppose I have to get used to the fact that Anchoterrias is yours now.'

'Not quite yet,' Eduardo corrected her quietly, and again she came under that steady and slightly unnerving scrutiny. 'Whether or not it ever does become mine depends on you, as you know, Lari.'

'Not entirely!' Lari denied a little breathlessly.

Eduardo leaned forward, looking down at the clasped hands between his knees for a second or two before he spoke. 'I don't demand an immediate answer from you, Lari, that wouldn't be reasonable, but you've had as long to consider the situation as I have, and you must realise that there's a limit to how much time we have.'

'Yes. Yes, I realise that.'

Before his arrival Lari had been sure in her mind that should he ask her to marry him, she would say yes without hesitation. But he had not really asked her in fact, and now that it came to the point she found herself too unsure of both the man and her own feelings for him. Initially, when the first shock of it was past, she had believed she could readily accept becoming Eduardo's wife; partly because her stepfather had wanted it that way, and partly because she knew how much Eduardo wanted Anchoterrias. But mostly because of a secret feeling she had nursed in her heart ever since she became old enough to be aware of him as a man. At fifteen, at their last meeting, she had come close to loving him, and it had been close enough for her not to denounce her stepfather's will as impossible to comply with.

'I don't want to rush you into something you're going to regret later,' Eduardo cautioned in a remarkably cool voice, and Lari looked up quickly. 'By marrying you I gain Anchoterrias and most of Tío José's estate, whereas you——' He lifted broad shoulders in a shrug. 'You might feel you gain little but the privilege of continuing to live in your old home, and going on as if nothing had happened.'

Lari would have given much to know what was going on behind that sternly cool expression. If she knew whether or not there was someone he would rather marry if only he could have Anchoterrias as well, it would help. He must be desperate at the thought of Anchoterrias going to a stranger unless he met with the conditions of his uncle's will and married her. He might even hate her behind that air of gentleness, because she had the power to deprive him of something that he had for years regarded as his inheritance: his uncle lacking a son.

'Oh—how can I know what you feel?' She spoke softly and breathlessly, aware as she got to her feet that Eduardo did so too, but remained standing beside his chair while she wandered restlessly across to the window. 'I wish I knew what *you* really want, Eduardo!'

'But you surely know that,' he said, and Lari turned from the view of endless vine-clad terraces to look at him. 'And you're my means of getting it, Lari.'

'Yes, I know.'

His singlemindedness chilled her, yet she told herself it was what she had known all along. Anchoterrias had belonged to the Sagreras for a very long time, always passing from father to eldest son, until tradition had been forced to sidestep when José Sagrera died childless. Lari had never really expected Eduardo to make a show of wanting her for any other reason than that she would bring him Anchoterrias; only her own indefinable feeling for him made her want it otherwise.

'Whatever you might think of me, Lari, I have to be honest—I'd marry the devil's daughter to get Anchoterrias, because it's been ours for too long for me to relish anyone else having it! Tío José in his wisdom made it impossible for me to get it without marrying you and giving you all the care and attention *he* gave you, and you have my word on it that I'll support and care for you just as he did.'

'I—I know you will.' She had known him too long not to believe him, but the thought of him in the role of guardian troubled her.

'If you decide against me the estate will go to whoever you marry, and that's something I can't even bear to think about.' He was silent for a moment, but the big room seemed to crackle with the high-charged emotion that held him tautly straight beside his chair. 'You said you wished you knew what I really want, Lari, and I'm telling you—I want Anchoterrias, just as I always have!'

Something stirred in Lari, making her hot and breathless; a feeling akin to anger but with much deeper implications, and she clenched her hands tightly at her side as she faced him. Her deep blue eyes appeared very nearly as dark as his, and they gleamed between their thick brown lashes as she kept her emotions tightly in check.

'At least you're honest about what your main interest is,' Lari told him, and she even managed a small tight smile. 'You don't pretend to be marrying me for any other reason than to get Anchoterrias!'

Anyone else, Lari felt, would have avoided her eyes at that point, but not so Eduardo Sagrera. He held her gaze boldly, causing little shivers of sensation to run over her skin like the evocative touch of fingertips. 'Don't decry yourself, Lari,' he told her. 'You've become a very lovely girl during the last six years, and I count that a bonus, though not entirely an unexpected one.'

To Lari the belated compliment was all too likely to have been made to placate her feminine vanity, and just for a moment she was tempted to tell him she *had* decided against him, and he wasn't going to get Anchoterrias after all. But it was too easy to remember the young man who had treated her gently when she was a small girl in a strange country, and much too hard to subdue her present awareness of the more mature and staggeringly attractive man he had become.

Marriage to Eduardo was what Papá had wanted for her, and it was what her own compulsive emotions demanded, so that she clasped her hands tightly together and gave him the answer he sought. 'I don't think I could live with the knowledge that I'd been responsible for Anchoterrias going out of the Sagrera family,' she said, and Eduardo looked at her steadily.

'You're very much younger than I am, Lari, but will you marry me?'

It was hard to meet the dark glowing look in his eyes and not be moved, and Lari hastily avoided them while she nodded agreement. 'I can't help feeling that that question should have been asked first,' she told him, 'but I'll make it possible for you to have Anchoterrias, Eduardo.' A small, tight smile reflected the bitterness she could not entirely conceal. 'I think you'll agree that the marriage is purely incidental!'

Shopping for her bridal outfit, Lari had to admit, was not as she had so often anticipated it, but then very little about her marriage to Eduardo was as she had always hoped it would be. Part of the trouble was that she was accompanied on the shopping trip by her future sister-in-law, who was helpful enough as far as it went, but showed none of the pleasure that would normally be expected of a young woman helping to choose the trousseau of her brother's bride.

Lari would much rather have gone alone, but to have refused the company of his sister would have offended Eduardo, she knew, even though she suspected he had arranged it so that she was chaperoned, as it were. In fact the dress she chose, as well as the narrow-brimmed straw hat she bought to go with it, met with approval.

Lari felt that the traditional long dress and veil would be out of place in the circumstances, but the outfit she chose was in the customary white nevertheless, except for a pale blue ribbon around the crown of the hat. Something blue, your love will be true, ran vaguely through her head, although she couldn't remember where she had heard it, and it was unlikely to be true in this case anyway, she told herself.

She raised no objections at all when her companion murmured an apology and left her to go off alone somewhere, arranging to meet on the ground floor of the store just before one o'clock closing. Left to her own devices, Lari relaxed a little more, and browsed around on her own until it was time to go.

There were very few people around, the floor she was on was almost deserted, and she hurried across to one of the elevators, hoping she had not left it too late. A flight of stairs began its descent alongside the gilded cage that stood already waiting for her, and she caught the slightly echoing sound of light footsteps on the stone stairs as she got in. Obviously someone preferred to walk.

Sliding the doors to, she jabbed a finger on the ground-floor button and stood back, curious for a moment when nothing happened except an odd crackling sound. Only a second later she went reeling back against the smooth wooden wall of the cage when it dropped a few feet and then jerked to a shuddering halt, her fingers scrabbling for a hold.

The floor of the department she had just left was now almost at eye level and with her heart in her mouth Lari looked out at as much of it as she could see. Her vision was limited by the proximity of a pair of slender legs that ended in expensive crocodile-skin shoes, and she took note, quite unthinkingly, of a small white scar that ran diagonally across the joint of one slim ankle.

Thanking heaven that someone was on hand to realise what had happened and to summon help, she called to the unseen woman while trying to make her appeal sound less anxious than she felt. There was no call for panic yet, and there were standard practices for dealing with emergencies like this, she felt sure.

'Will you get help, please, *señora*! The lift has

stuck and I don't—I'm afraid it might drop down further if someone doesn't do something.'

She had no doubt at all that her plea had been heard, for there was something about the stance of those elegant feet that suggested she had their owner's attention, and yet she got no reply. No one bent to look at her or to check and see if she was all right. Instead she caught something she could not quite believe; a brief and barely audible expression of satisfaction; and almost immediately after that the feet turned and disappeared from her sight.

Clinging to the metal lattice-work gate of the lift, Lari tried to see something, but she heard only the sharp clicking of high heels on the stone stairway right next to the lift, and her heart began a rapid urgent beat that was close to panic. How could anyone, she wondered, ignore a possible serious accident and simply walk away? On reflection she allowed that the woman might have gone for help after all; that made more sense—it was also less frightening.

Scarcely had she begun to console herself with the thought when she gasped in sudden terror when the lift creaked ominously before plummeting downward and throwing her completely off balance. Only briefly it came to a jarring halt, then once more pitched downward with Lari screaming long and loud in blind terror as she sought in vain for something to cling to.

Shaken and terrified, she was hurled across the width of the polished floor helplessly and brought up against the far wall with a sickening crack that left her dazed and trembling. She shook her head to try and clear it, but realised her mistake when it throbbed like a drum. Sheer terror brought a bitter taste into her mouth and made her stomach heave with nausea, so that she barely noticed for a moment that the lift had again come to a stop.

How long she stayed without moving Lari had no

idea, but she felt almost afraid to breathe for fear of starting that nightmare ride again, and she roused herself only when a man's voice came echoing down the lift shaft. It was flattened and dulled by the confined space, but despite its hint of panic it was reassuring, and she was badly in need of reassurance.

'*Señora?*' The mistaken assumption was a natural one, she allowed. '*Señora*, can you hear me? I beg of you, don't move an inch!'

'I won't!' Lari doubted very much if her voice would reach the man above, and she dared not move to make herself heard for she could all too easily imagine the dire result if she did. 'Please—please *do* something!'

A murmur of voices reached her, and Lari bit hard on her lip when the lift shifted just a fraction more. It was dark between floors, for the overhead light had failed when the lift went out of control, and she had never felt more afraid in her life as she crouched against the shiny wooden wall of her prison, chewing anxiously on her thumb nail and listening.

'Help is coming, *señora*!' the reassuring voice reached her again, and thankfully sounded more confident. 'Keep quite still, *señora*, and don't worry. It will take time, but we'll have you out of there, I promise you!'

There was another jumble of voices, wordless and annoyingly indecipherable to Lari, then the thinner, lighter sound of a woman's voice penetrated the jumble and reached her quite clearly. 'Be sure and remain still,' it admonished. 'Eduardo will be here directly.'

'Oh no!' However loudly Lari said it, she doubted if it reached her well-meaning sister-in-law. She was not, it seemed, prepared to bear the incident alone and had sent for her brother as the more interested party. 'You shouldn't have——' she began, then sighed resignedly. Even if her words were audible, they would go unheeded, for the Sagreras heeded no wishes but their own.

'Don't move!' the voice repeated, and Lari shook her head, 'and don't worry.'

Lari had no intention of moving an inch if she could help it, but how anyone in her situation could not worry, she didn't know. Her legs were already cramped from being curled up under her, and her head ached appallingly where she had hit it against the wall when she fell.

Judging by the sounds that reached her there was a great deal of activity going on, but the wait seemed interminable, and while she fretted and grew more and more uncomfortable with the passing of time, she pondered on what Eduardo would have to say about his precious bride being put in danger. Not precious in the romantic sense, she hastened to remind herself, but very precious as the key to Anchoterrias.

Crouched as she was, she dared not try and stretch her legs for fear of inducing another plunge downward, and she seemed to have been there for hours when a more familiar voice called echoingly down the lift shaft to her. 'Lari?' Her heart thudded so hard she felt sure it must jolt the precariously balanced cage, and she hadn't a hope of making him hear her if she called back from her present position. 'Lari? Are you all right?'

His voice reached her amid a clatter of bangs and scraping noises, and she had to recognise the anxiety in it. Drawing as deep a breath as she dared, she called back to him.

'I'm all right!'

'I can just hear your voice,' he called, more loudly than before which suggested he had leaned further out into the shaft. 'Just keep quite still, Lari, and you'll be O.K.'

Keep still. That was all the advice she had been

given, and her growing irritability owed itself to a head that pounded relentlessly and legs that were becoming numb with cramp. Leaning back against the wall, she closed her eyes for a moment, trying to keep herself calm by remembering that she must thank the woman in the crocodile shoes who had evidently given the warning after all.

Her eyes flicked swiftly open again when she realised that the lift was moving. Not the jerky uncontrolled plunge downward like before, but a slower, smoother ascent that suggested lifting gear had been brought into action; and without her being altogether aware of it, tears formed in her eyes and rolled down her cheeks.

She was still crouched in the same spot, dazed and with tears in her eyes, when the metal gates crashed back and she was exposed to the gaze of a small group of people gathered around the opening. It was Eduardo who reached for her hands and helped her to her feet. Gentle as he had always been and anxious too, and with such a look in his eyes that she knew he had been concerned for her and not simply because she was to bring him Anchoterrias.

'Lari!' The moment they were on solid ground he drew her into his arms and one big hand cradled her aching head to his chest while his fingers stroked lightly over her heair. 'It's all over now, Lari, don't cry, little one, it's all over.' He let her rest there for a moment or two, then he eased her away and looked down into her face, his dark gaze sweeping over pale cheeks and the growing shadow of a bruise on her forehead. 'There's a doctor coming to look at you, and the moment he says you're O.K. we can go home, hmm?'

Oh, how familiar that gentle, kindly concern was, Lari thought, and found no fault with it even now she was much older and soon to become his wife. Eduardo knew just how to gentle her, to make her feel better; there was something about him that hadn't changed at all. But she did not like the idea of a doctor having been called, and frowned over it.

'Eduardo, I don't need a doctor,' she told him. 'I only have a headache, that's all.'

'Nevertheless,' Eduardo said, kindly but adamant, 'you'll see him and make quite sure. Thank heaven I was in Seville and Elena knew where to find me. What on earth possessed you to do such a silly thing, Lari?'

Completely at a loss, but sensing criticism, Lari brushed a hand across her eyes and frowned at him curiously. 'I—I don't know what you mean, Eduardo. The lift broke down, but that was nothing to do with anything I did.'

From the corner of her eye she was aware of people exchanging glances, then one of them stepped forward, rubbing his hands together and looking slightly embarrassed. A short stout man in a dark suit, he glanced at Eduardo before addressing her. 'But the lift was quite clearly marked as out of order, *señorita.* Any of the people here will support what I say.'

Lari was too stunned for a moment to take it in and she simply stared at him blankly. Then Eduardo turned her round slowly so that she could see the gleaming wooden box she had just escaped from; the few spectators who remained moved back so that she had an uninterrupted view and he pointed to the call button beside the cage. A rectangle of card swung from it, clearly visible and with a red zig-zag across its width with the words, *Danger—Do Not Use!*

Lari stared at it for several seconds, willing herself to remember the few moments before she stepped into the lift, and she was certain that there had been no notice there then. Not hanging from the call button as it did now, or anywhere else in sight. She couldn't possibly have overlooked it if it had been there.

'It wasn't there.' She spoke so softly that initially no one but Eduardo heard what she said, then more insistently and looking at the man in the dark suit when she said it. 'I swear that notice wasn't there when I got into the lift! I *know* it wasn't there!'

'Lari!' He eased her on to the chair someone brought, gently reproachful.

'It was hung there last evening, *señorita,*' the man assured her, and looked more sad than angered by her insistence.

Eduardo took her hand, squeezing her fingers while he spoke. 'Lari, you're mistaken; all these people saw it there, last evening and this morning, as Señor Magara says. You just couldn't have noticed it. Maybe you were—distracted by your shopping and the nearness of closing time.'

His making excuses for her almost made it worse, for there was a chill flutter of unease in her stomach that was too disturbing to ignore, and she moistened her lips hastily before she replied. 'I *swear* it wasn't there, Eduardo!' A brief recollection of slender legs and crocodile shoes flashed before her mind's eye, and she turned to him eagerly. 'The woman who called for help,' she said. 'She was standing there, she must have noticed the card wasn't there!'

'It was Señorita Franciscus of our lingerie department who heard your screams and summoned assistance, *señorita,*' the man informed her, and indicated a short stout woman built along the same lines as he was himself, and who was very unlikely ever to have owned a pair of expensive crocodile shoes.

'No, no, there was another woman,' Lari insisted. 'She was standing by the lift just after it stuck for the first time, and she was wearing crocodile shoes. I could only see her feet,' she explained hastily, 'but she was standing close and I asked her to get help, only——'

Her voice tapered off when she remembered that barely audible sigh of satisfaction and something crawled across her scalp and slid along her spine; something cold and shiver-inducing. No one was going to believe her, that much was clear, for the manager of the store was already shaking his head slowly and there was a tighter look about Eduardo's mouth that she took heed of, so that she gazed from one to the other in despair.

'Assistance was summoned by Señorita Franciscus, *señorita,*' the manager assured her, and he had no illusions about the kind of shoes his staff could afford. 'There was no lady such as you describe anywhere in sight when you called for help.'

Lari looked around at the people who encircled her as she sat on a straight-backed wooden chair with Eduardo's hand on her shoulder, and she was filled with a sense of panic again suddenly without being quite sure why. Some were a little wary, most sympathetic but unconvinced, and there was an unexplained fear growing in the back of her mind that refused to be dismissed.

Eduardo's explanation looked so convincing on the face of it. She had been thinking about her coming wedding and the thrill of buying her wedding gown, and she had not noticed the warning sign on the lift. And yet she knew in her heart that it hadn't been there, and that the woman in the crocodile-skin shoes had.

Eduardo's hand stroked gently down her cheek suddenly, and she looked up at him, affected by his gentleness as she always was, and almost desperate that he should believe her if no one else did. 'You don't believe me,' she said, not bothering to make it a question, and he put an arm around her shoulders, drawing her close for a moment.

'You were frightened,' he said in his most persuasive voice, and she knew he was still making excuses for her. 'I've sent Elena back to her own family, but the minute the doctor's O.K.'d you I'll drive you back to

Anchoterrias and tell Marta to take care of you.'

Lari didn't answer, but shook her head slowly. Her legs were shaking even though she was sitting down, and she wasn't sure of anything any more. Above her head, Eduardo was murmuring something to the manager and she clenched her hands tightly at the thought of him apologising for her, then the moment they were alone for a few seconds before the doctor arrived, she did her best to try again to convince him.

'Eduardo, you must believe me, there *was* a woman there, and I *did* ask her to go for help. I swear there was no notice on the lift, and I don't care whether or not you believe me,' she went on when he opened his mouth to say something, 'I saw her standing there and if she didn't call for help then——'

The full implication of what she was saying struck her suddenly and she caught her lower lip between her teeth, her heart thudding hard. Looking down at her, Eduardo was obviously more in sympathy than angry with her persistence, and yet she thought there was a hint of impatience in the deep soothing voice. 'Lari, you've had a bang on the head——'

'But I'm not wandering in my mind!'

A long-drawn sigh suggested he was running out of patience, but he was still incredibly gentle and quiet when he spoke. 'My dear child, who on earth would want to harm you in the way you're implying?'

'I don't know—of course I don't know!' She put a hand to her aching head. So many things whirled around in her mind and confused her and there was nothing she could do about them. One thing she could do something about and hastened to do so was his manner of addressing her, and she spoke without hesitation. 'And I hope you don't intend making a habit of calling me your child,' she told him sharply. 'I was under the impression you were marrying me to get Anchoterrias, Eduardo, not adopting me!'

He turned his dark eyes on her and they were deep and fathomless, sending little shivers of sensation fluttering along her spine. 'At the moment,' he informed her, 'if there was another way of getting what is rightfully mine, I wouldn't be doing either!'

Lari felt small, confused and very uncertain of anything, and when she looked up at him her eyes were wide and appealing, for Eduardo had never shown her anything but kindness until now. 'I wish there was some other way too,' she whispered reproachfully.

But she knew even before his fingers tightened their hold on hers that she had not meant it. Having Anchoterrias meant having Eduardo too, and that somehow seemed to have been destined ever since she could remember.

CHAPTER TWO

IT was just three weeks after the incident in the lift that Lari and Eduardo were married, and she had been so busy in the time between that she had little chance to dwell on the mystery of what had really happened. Had it not been for that mysterious woman in the crocodile-skin shoes, she might almost have believed that Eduardo was right, and she had simply not noticed the warning card on the lift because she was too preoccupied with other matters.

In a number of ways Lari's wedding was reminiscent of her mother's to José Sagrera eleven years before, for the same group of relatives who had attended on that occasion also attended hers and Eduardo's. Just as then a quiet ceremony was followed by a small reception at Anchoterrias, and quite clearly in some cases, another English bride in their ranks was no more welcome than the first had been.

Lari made an enchanting bride in a calf-length dress of Almagro lace and the white straw hat, and Eduardo did not hesitate to remark on it. 'You look lovely,' he told her after the last of their guests had arrived and been greeted with champagne. 'But I still find it hard to believe that you're grown up enough to be a bride. You still look very much like the schoolgirl I knew six years ago.'

With memories of her former almost painful thinness, Lari found it hard to believe that a man such as she judged Eduardo to be, could not have noticed at least that much change in her. But she smiled at the compliment, whatever its reservations. 'I hope I don't look exactly like I did when I was fifteen,' she told him with an upward glance from the corner of her eye. 'I was such a skinny creature at that age.'

Very deliberately his eyes strayed down to the soft curves that the lace dress revealed so flatteringly, and they lingered for long enough to bring a swift colour to her cheeks before a slight nod acknowledged the transformation. 'Of course you're no longer skinny, if you ever were,' he agreed, 'but there's still a certain—naïveté about you that shows how closely Tío José sheltered you from life.'

To Lari it wasn't the remark of a doting bridegroom, and she questioned him hastily and a little anxiously, 'Do you intend to go on sheltering me, Eduardo?'

While they held hers for a long moment Eduardo's dark eyes were shadowed by their thick lashes and quite unfathomable. 'It's what I've undertaken to do in return for Anchoterrias,' he reminded her quietly. 'At least until you're—mature.' She would have risen indignantly to the defence of her maturity, but he had turned his head as he spoke and was already detached from the subject. 'I can see my father calling me across to talk to an old friend,' he said. 'Will family reminiscences bore you too much?'

In the circumstances, the prospect of family gossip had little appeal, and Lari shook her head, more uneasy about his attitude than she cared to admit. 'You go by all means,' she told him, 'but I'll stay here; I'm sure you'll enjoy reminiscing more without me standing around. I'll be perfectly all right,' she hastened to assure him when he hesitated. 'I shall have some more champagne!'

Still he lingered, as if he genuinely disliked the idea of leaving her, then he shrugged lightly before turning to answer his father's summons. 'If you'd rather—I won't be very long.' He looked at her and half-smiled, his eyes showing that old familiar gentleness that in this instance somehow seemed less comforting than irritating. 'Don't drink too much champagne, little one!'

How long he expected to be, Lari didn't know, but he was gone for much longer than she had anticipated, and in the very formal atmosphere among her Sagrera relatives she began to feel like a stranger at her own wedding. She was close to the refreshment table that held the drinks and she was already on her fourth glass of champagne as a means of consolation when she felt someone was watching her.

It was a tingling, irresistible sensation, feeling herself under observation, and she turned slowly round to find herself the subject of an intensive and frankly appreciative scrutiny by a fair-haired young man. He stood just a little further along the table and he too was drinking champagne, smiling at her over the rim of his glass and raising it in a toast as she turned.

'Isn't it customary for the bridegroom to be standing guard on his new bride?' he asked, and Lari was briefly startled by the fact that he spoke English with an obviously native accent. He moved along, coming to stand closer, and the smiling grey eyes never moved from her face, as if the sight of it enthralled him. 'And you should never be left unguarded, Señora Sagrera!'

Lari hadn't the faintest idea who he might be, and she gazed at him a little blankly, trying to recall a name. 'I'm sorry, *señor*——'

'Oh, I wasn't invited,' he informed her with no apparent embarrassment, 'so I gatecrashed your wedding breakfast in the hope of being able to drown my sorrow in your champagne.' He took a long drink from his glass and again fixed his eyes on her with that same intense gaze. 'I was away only a couple of weeks, back in England,' he told her, 'and I came back only to find you married!'

His meaning was unmistakable, and Lari flushed as she answered in what had once been her native tongue, but which she now spoke with a slight Spanish accent.

'I'm sorry, but I don't recognise you, *señor.*'

'Why should you?' he asked, pulling a face. 'My name is Eric Truman and I've lived next to you for the past six months, but I doubt if you've even noticed my existence. I write books,' he added with a faintly ironic smile, and the name at last registered with Lari.

'Oh, but of course I've heard of you, Señor Truman!'

'Señor Truman.' He echoed her accent as well as her words. 'You've been in Spain a long time?' he guessed. 'I'd thought of you as being English, but your accent—you seem so much more Spanish than I expected.'

He was a disconcerting man, and not least because he gazed at her so intently, but she did not see how she could simply walk off and leave him in the circumstances. Besides which she had no one else to talk to, and he at least wasn't a Sagrera who resented her hold on Anchoterrias.

'I came to Spain when I was only ten years old,' Lari explained, 'and I count myself a Spaniard now, *señor.*'

'More so than ever now that you have a Spanish husband, I imagine,' he guessed, and Lari inclined her head without verbally committing herself on the subject.

Eric Truman laughed shortly and seemingly without reason, then he put down his empty glass on the table behind her. He was as tall as Eduardo, but fair and very good-looking, and he was something outside her experience of her native Englishman. There was boldness about him that was more Latin than Anglo-Saxon and just for a moment as he leaned across behind her he was close enough for the warmth of his body to penetrate her lace wedding dress. Only partially straightening up, he looked directly into her eyes.

'What happens now?' he challenged. 'Do you have

me thrown out on my ear as a trespasser?'

A little lightheaded with the champagne she had consumed, Lari was briefly at a loss, but coped as best she could with a completely alien experience. 'Of course I shan't have you thrown out, *señor,*' she denied hastily. 'The Spanish are hospitable people by tradition, and you are welcome to stay and have some more champagne.'

Quite clearly it was the answer he had expected, for when he turned back with his glass refilled, he was still smiling and seemed perfectly at ease. 'Do you realise how long I've been fancying you from a distance?' he asked, and Lari's eyes went instinctively in search of Eduardo.

He was no longer in the company of his father, but now stood in what appeared to be a very earnest and confidential discussion with a woman whom Lari had noticed particularly when they were introduced after the ceremony. It had been she, Lari felt convinced, whom Eduardo had referred to as an old friend.

Dark and handsome in the style of the Andaluz, she had huge eyes and a bold smile, with silky black hair bound up into the traditional chignon. She was modern in every other aspect, however, including the *haute couture* suit she wore, and Lari remembered her name was Juana Cortez.

'Ah, you've noticed!'

The English voice spoke close to her ear, and Lari had no doubt at all what it was implying. There was a wild clamouring in her heart that she fought to subdue, but it was hard to ignore the fact that Eduardo had stayed to continue his conversation with the Spanish woman after the rest of their group had drifted away.

'He must be mad!' Eric Truman declared unhesitatingly.

'Señor Truman——'

'I know, I know, it's none of my business!' He held up a hand, and his smile was so completely disarming that Lari could not pretend to blame him for long. 'I'm sorry,' he told her. 'I know it isn't anything to do with me, but for the life of me I just can't see how any man with a bride as lovely as you can leave her to go and talk to another woman.'

Lari had no intention of putting him in the picture concerning the nature of her marriage to Eduardo, but she appreciated his obviously genuine resentment on her behalf. Colour warmed her cheeks and some of it, she knew, was due to the amount of champagne she had consumed, but not all. There was something about the good-looking man beside her that gave her morale the boost it needed in view of Eduardo's preoccupation with the handsome and sultry Juana Cortez.

'Señora Cortez is an old friend of my husband's,' she told Eric Truman, 'and I've no doubt they have a lot to talk about.'

'Really?' The implication was unmistakable and Lari frowned uneasily.

Although an over-indulgence in champagne had made her slightly less cautious than usual, she tried to make it as plain as she possibly could and still be polite, that she didn't want to discuss the matter of her husband's companion. 'I think it's time I circulated a little, if you'll excuse me,' she said. 'There's plenty of drink, Señor Truman, and *tapas* on the other table if you'd like something to eat with it. Please help yourself.'

'You're not going to have me thrown out, then?'

He had never seriously expected her to, Lari thought, but he was an oddly disturbing guest as well as an unexpected one to find at her wedding reception. She still wasn't quite sure how to react to him or how seriously to take him. 'You're welcome to stay as long as you wish, *señor*, of course.'

In fact Lari had little intention of circulating as she

had said, but of seeking the less formal air of the *patio* where she could enjoy a few moments' respite without being observed. There were one or two people already out there, but Lari knew of quiet corners where she was unlikely to be seen and where she could find solitude among the scented shrubs and trees.

She was in the act of stepping through the open door on to the *patio* when a voice murmured close to her ear in English, 'May I come with you, wherever you're going?'

'Señor Truman——'

'It was to see you, I came,' he pointed out, 'and you don't really mind, do you?'

Hesitating in the doorway still, Lari wasn't sure how to reply. There was no fear that Eduardo would be jealous, she could almost wish he would be, but the Sagreras were firm in their family pride and she was the wife of one of them. Eduardo's tête-à-tête with Juana Cortez might be acceptable as a man's privilege, but any indiscretion on her part, however slight, would be less readily overlooked. Big towns like Seville might have eased their code into the more relaxed atmosphere of the times, but in the country districts tradition died much harder.

'I don't think it would be a very good idea, *señor,*' she told him a little anxiously, but even while she said it, Eric Truman was looking back over his shoulder to where Eduardo was still listening with apparent interest to what his companion was saying.

'I don't think your husband will miss you,' he suggested. 'Do you?'

There was bright colour in her cheeks and Lari felt a curious churning sensation inside her when she looked at Juana Cortez, smiling up so intimately into Eduardo's face, and for the first time in her life she felt a twinge of jealousy. Whether or not theirs was a marriage of convenience only, he surely owed her the courtesy of remaining with her on their wedding day. If he didn't then he could hardly complain if she played him at his own game.

With a light toss of her head that slightly dislodged her straw hat, Lari walked out into the sunshine, and she did nothing at all to deter him when Eric Truman came with her. She was aware that a couple of Sàgrera aunts watched, with their sharp black eyes on him, but she chose to ignore the possible consequences if they informed Eduardo. There was a place at the rear of the house that was quieter and more private, giving an endless vista of vines on a hot sunny hillside, and she went directly there, welcoming the shade of a fringe of palms that protected it from the sun.

It wasn't somewhere she would have normally brought a stranger, and particularly a strange man who had gatecrashed her wedding reception, but on this occasion nothing was normal, and an over-indulgence in champagne had made her less cautious than usual. She pulled off her hat and shook back her hair, but for the moment she didn't look at her companion. Eric Truman had become unimportant in his own right and merely existed as a sounding board for her own unfamiliar mood.

'There are too many people in there,' she complained. 'I prefer it when there's just the two of us.'

'You and your husband?'

Lari turned swiftly at the soft-voiced enquiry, for it brought home to her that she would never again share Anchoterrias with her stepfather. And the sudden hurt she felt showed in her eyes and sobered her wine-fuddled head as nothing else could have done. 'I was thinking of Papá,' she said huskily. 'I'm sorry, *señor*, I had no intention of involving you.'

'I don't think I ever really saw him,' Eric Truman told her, smoothly interrupting her apology. 'I saw you drive past sometimes with a man in the front seat beside you, but I never really knew who he was.'

'It was my stepfather. He likes—liked to go for a drive sometimes.'

'And you miss him a lot, don't you?'

There was a kind of gentleness about him suddenly that reminded her of Eduardo, and how gently he had probed for the interest of a little English girl; trying to draw her out when she was shy and unsure of a man who spoke a strange tongue. She had a sudden need for Eduardo that she did not altogether understand when she remembered that he was with another woman, and unlikely to be interested enough to come and look for his bride.

'I miss him,' she agreed huskily, and caught her breath when she realised how close he had come.

'And you need someone to talk to about him.'

Lari could not imagine how his arm came to be around her shoulders, or how he came to be standing with his head bent and his face just lightly brushing against her hair. 'Señor Truman,' she protested breathlessly, 'I don't——'

'Oh, why in God's name didn't I come sooner!' he asked in a voice that was raspingly harsh and emotional. 'If I had maybe you wouldn't be—— Damn it, I was trying to be polite, do it all by the book, and look where it got me! I come back after a couple of weeks and you're married!'

Lari understood only part of what he was saying, but she felt it was something she should object to and she was about to do so when he bent and kissed her neck just below her left ear, a soft vulnerable spot that pulsed rapidly after the caress. Neither of them was aware of another presence until a deep and familiar voice, hard and flat with suspicion, brought Lari's head up sharply and caused the immediate withdrawal of the arm around her shoulders.

'I came to see where you'd got to, Lari,' Eduardo

ignored the stranger for the moment apart from a very brief inclination of his head, and Lari noticed that he made no attempt to avoid her eyes. Had he done so she felt it would have been an admission of his own shortcomings, but instead he held her gaze with the familiar bold and steady look that she always found so disturbing. 'Have you forgotten we have guests?'

Lari's colour flared at the unmistakable reprimand, and answering him in English instead of Spanish was quite deliberate, although it obviously surprised him. 'Of course I haven't forgotten, Eduardo, but I needed some fresh air; unlike you I'm not accustomed to a house full of people.' She turned to the man beside her. 'This is Señor Eric Truman who has the property next to ours. Señor Truman, may I introduce my husband, Eduardo Sagrera.'

'You are English, *señor*?'

It was years since she had heard Eduardo speak English and it was much more pedantic and strongly accented than her own, naturally, but what surprised her most was how well he spoke it. As a child she had often had difficulty understanding him. Quite clearly his arrogance, indeed his whole bearing, made Eric Truman uneasy, but Lari also noticed an unmistakable gleam of resentment in his eyes as he shook hands.

'I hope you'll forgive my gatecrashing to meet a compatriot, Señor Sagrera,' he said. 'I've had it in mind to come over and pay my respects for some time, but I understood that the late Señor Sagrera was something of a recluse, and I didn't like to intrude.'

'Your consideration does you credit, *señor,*' Eduardo assured him gravely. 'It was most courteous of you to bring us your good wishes today. A glass of champagne, perhaps? There is plenty in the house and you are welcome to it.'

Eric Truman's eyes sought Lari's vainly, and his smile was not nearly as confident as it had been earlier.

'Thank you,' he said, 'but I've already had champagne.'

'Ah!' Not by so much as a blink did Eduardo betray how he felt; his manner and his features were, as always, perfectly under control. 'Then if you arrived by way of the *viña, señor,* please allow me to save you a long hot walk back by providing you with transport.'

It was unmistakably a dismissal but still formally polite, and whether or not their uninvited guest had come by way of the vineyard, Lari had no idea. That he resented being sent packing showed only in his eyes as they darted swiftly between Lari and Eduardo, as if he looked to her to countermand the suggestion.

Lari was in two minds about it. She acknowledged a certain unexpected pleasure at the idea of Eduardo being so anxious to see off her admirer, but on the other hand it was quite likely his precious Sagrera pride that made him do it, not because he cared about her. Also she disliked him getting things all his own way, and it was very doubtful if Juana Cortez was being dismissed so uncompromisingly.

'Señor Truman is my guest, Eduardo,' she told him, her pique unmistakable. 'Surely you don't mind me having one compatriot at my wedding, do you?'

Eduardo's near-black eyes darkened perceptibly, but his control as always was unfailing. 'I beg your pardon, *señor,*' he said quietly, 'I must have misunderstood you earlier. Of course you are welcome to join our other guests, but I feel I must deprive you of my wife's company—you understand?'

'Oh, perfectly, *señor*!' Eric Truman's half-smile verged on the insolent, but he too kept up an appearance of good manners, and even managed a slight bow. 'As a matter of fact I was about to leave, but I won't take advantage of the lift, thanks very much; I'll go back the way I came.' Reaching for Lari's hand, he raised it to his lips and kissed her fingers, retaining his hold for a fraction longer than politeness demanded. 'Goodbye, Señora Segrera, I'm glad to have met you at last, though I wish I'd come sooner.' He sighed deeply with apparently genuine regret. 'Oh well, may I hope we meet again some time?'

From the corner of her eye Lari noticed the arrogant angle of Eduardo's head and the frown that gathered his black brows. 'Some time, perhaps, *señor,*' he said, answering before she had time to answer for herself. 'In the meantime will you excuse us? Our other guests —*adios, señor!*'

The other man hesitated only fractionally, then inclined his head briefly and turned away, while Lari, hatless and pink-cheeked, watched him out of sight. She turned swiftly when hard fingers gripped her upper arm, noting with some misgiving the firm line of Eduardo's mouth. 'I assume you have some explanation for your extraordinary behaviour?' he said, in the more familiar Spanish, and Lari eyed him warily. 'Although I can't imagine what reason you can have for sneaking off from your own wedding reception with some man you don't know and hiding in the most private part of the garden!'

She tugged her arm free and shook back her hair, looking up at him more in reproach than anger. 'I didn't think you'd miss me,' she told him, 'you were so busy with Señora Cortez.'

It was hard to believe that he was even slightly put out, and yet that was the impression Lari got. 'I explained that she was an old friend, Lari, and I could hardly just walk away while she was talking.'

Lari nodded. 'I didn't quite understand who she was—is—exactly. Is she a relation?'

Eduardo, she realised, was regarding her with slightly narrowed eyes and clearly Juana Cortez was the last person he wanted to discuss. 'In fact she is the widow of my mother's cousin's son,' he told her eventually.

'Oh, a *close* relation!' Sarcasm was not natural to her and Lari was rather surprised to realise that she was using it to goad him quite deliberately.

'Don't be childish, Lari!' His mouth tightened again into an ominously hard line. 'The fact that I was having a private conversation with a member of my family is no reason for you to sneak off——'

'Will you stop saying I *sneaked* off!' Lari demanded. 'Most of the people in the *salón* saw me go, and I know Tía Maria and Tía Enriqueta saw me; I guessed they'd tell you!' Her look challenged him to deny the source of his information, and to Eduardo's credit he didn't attempt to.

'They told me they'd seen you coming this way with a man they'd never seen before,' he told her. 'They were concerned and, naturally, so was I.'

'Concerned for me?' Lari asked, unable to resist it. 'Or for the reputation of the Sagreras?'

She hastily avoided the look she saw in his eyes suddenly, and felt very small. Not that she was prepared to admit she had done anything to be ashamed of, she could still recall him in intimate conversation with Juana Cortez, but because Eduardo had the ability to make her feel that she was still the little English girl he had first known eleven years ago.

'I was under the impression that we shared that reputation now that you're my wife,' he suggested quietly. Reaching for her hands, he held them while he studied her for a second or two in silence. 'Did you know him before today, Lari; this Englishman? Does he—matter to you?'

Lari wondered what he would have done if she had answered in the affirmative, but she found herself incapable of that kind of deception. 'I never met him until today,' she said. 'And he told the truth when he said he gatecrashed the reception; he told *me* he did.'

Eduardo still held her hands and his thumbs were

moving slowly back and forth over the pulse at her wrist, a slow, stroking, strangely erotic caress that stirred her senses alarmingly, while he looked down at her thoughtfully. 'And yet I'd swear he—admires you,' he murmured, almost as if to himself. 'He spoke of wanting to come over and see you even before Tío José died, so it appears he's been here for some time.'

'Six months. He told me that too,' she added hastily. 'But I've never seen him until today.'

A faintly derisive smile gave his mouth that suggestion of cruelty she had noticed once before. 'Apparently he took more interest in you than you have in him,' Eduardo suggested. 'He had every appearance of a man very badly smitten, and the fact that he makes little effort to conceal it makes me realise I shall have to take him very seriously.' He turned her about until they were facing the house, then tucked a hand under her arm and guided her back along the path. 'I must keep it in mind that you have such a fervent admirer, and you must remember that you're now my wife.'

Glancing up, Lari studied the strong dark features intently for a second, remembering again his attentiveness towards Juana Cortez. 'Just as long as *you* remember it!' she retorted pertly, and gasped aloud when she was pulled around in front of him suddenly and held tight against the lean hard length of him.

Bending his head, he kissed the soft spot just below her ear with a touch so light it was barely more than a breath on her skin. 'Oh, I will!' he promised.

Lari's first day as a bride was not at all as she had always visualised it. Not that she could claim that marrying Eduardo had been merely compliance with an old man's will, even though it appeared to be little more on the surface, for she had always loved Anchoterrias and in her heart she knew it would take very little to make her love Eduardo too. On the face of it they had both done reasonably well from the marriage, for Eduardo had what he wanted and, in part, so had she.

What struck Lari most forcibly, coming downstairs that first morning, was the feeling of dissatisfaction she had with the way things were. It had begun last night and grown this morning when Eduardo had walked past her bedroom door without even pausing to knock and ask if she was ready to join him for breakfast. The first breakfast for a newly married couple, she felt, should have a cosy, intimate air with the accent on shared whispers and kisses. It should be more than merely the uneventful meeting of two people converging from their separate rooms like guests at an hotel.

The *patio* was filled with the scents of morning and her mood lifted a little when she caught sight of Eduardo sitting at the table laid for two under the orange trees, despite the initial shock of seeing him in the place that her stepfather had occupied for so long. His dark head was bent over a newspaper he was seemingly engrossed in and it gave her undeniable pleasure to remind herself that he was her husband.

A white shirt emphasised broad shoulders and bare brown arms, and she felt a curious curling sensation in her stomach that was inexplicable when she remembered how they had gone last night to their separate rooms, after saying goodnight with nothing more than a light, brief kiss. Nothing would change, Eduardo had assured her, as if convinced it was what she wanted to hear.

At fifteen years old she had secretly dreamed of the kind of husband Eduardo would be and, in the way of young girls, she had imagined him a virile and exciting lover. She had never in her wildest dreams visualised him kissing her goodnight at her bedroom door and leaving her to go to his own solitary bed, as he had last night. It was an unsatisfactory situation, and one she had to admit she had not allowed for when she agreed to marry him.

Her feet made little sound on the sun-warmed stones, and she was within touching distance before Eduardo looked up and saw her, but the moment he did he was on his feet, moving with that peculiarly cat-like grace he possessed. When he pushed in her chair she was enveloped for a moment in the warm intimacy of his body and her senses responded wildly, so that when he pressed another of those coolly impassive kisses on her cheek it was like ice after fire.

'Good morning, Lari, did you sleep well?'

Such cool formality made it irresistible to answer as she did. 'Oh yes, thank you, Eduardo, just as I always do.'

She sensed his watching her when she reached for the coffee pot and she could guess that his eyes would be narrowed slightly, and speculative, as she had noticed them before; not quite sure of her meaning. Somehow it gave her a certain satisfaction to realise that she could even slightly disturb that air of cool composure.

'Is your room comfortable?' she enquired, and thought how much more like a polite hostess she sounded than a newly married wife. 'Marta thought you'd like the end room, it's bigger.'

Eduardo was spreading honey on a roll with deliberate care, and he spoke quietly, yet something in his tone caught Lari's attention and made her look up quickly and frown. 'Was it Marta who decided which room I was to have?'

Lari shrugged, uncertain but suspicious. 'Well—yes, of course.'

The roll, dripping honey, was poised before his mouth and his eyes were half hidden by incredibly thick black lashes. 'Not of course, Lari; it isn't the housekeeper's job to allocate rooms.' When she didn't answer, the quiet voice went on inexorably. 'Incidentally, I'd prefer to have the master bedroom from now on: I'm surprised Marta didn't think of it, but perhaps you'll see that she's informed, will you?'

Lari eyed him for a moment in silence, for her emotions were too tangled for her to think clearly. It shouldn't really have come as a shock to think of him taking over her stepfather's room as well as his place at the table, but somehow it did. 'You mean Papá's room?' she asked, and watched the honeyed roll disappear into his mouth with a kind of fascination.

'I imagine it was,' Eduardo agreed smoothly. 'It's customary for the master bedroom to be——'

'Occupied by the master! Oh yes, of course, I understand!'

He regarded her steadily while he removed the stickiness of honey from his lips with the tip of his tongue, and Lari's pulse pounded like a drum as she coped with unfamiliar emotions. 'Don't you like the idea?' he asked, and the challenge was unmistakable.

Whether or not she actively disliked it, Lari couldn't have said for certain, but his demand to be given the master bedroom seemed somehow to stress his authority; and at a moment when it was still hard to see him as her stepfather's substitute. 'You're entitled to it,' she allowed, but didn't commit herself beyond that.

Eduardo inclined his head in brief acknowledgment of the fact, and continued to eat in silence for a moment or two. Then he poured himself more coffee and sat with his hands clasping the big patterned cup while he looked across at her. 'I'm wondering, Lari; does Marta also make up the menus and decide which wines we drink?'

'Why, yes.' As she went on she wished she could follow his train of thought more closely. 'We mostly drink our own, of course, but we have quite a lot of Santa Inés too. Papá always said that the only one who could make wine as good as that of Anchoterrias was his brother—your father.'

Eduardo acknowledged the compliment gravely. 'We have a good reputation,' he agreed, then returned firmly to the subject he seemed determined to settle. 'The menu and the wine we had at dinner last night, did Marta also choose those?'

Again Lari nodded, but she was eyeing him warily. Her heart was beating hard and she wasn't sure why, except that she was certain something was about to change that she hadn't anticipated. 'Yes, of course she did, Eduardo, Marta's always run the house. She's very capable and the rest of the staff like her; it isn't easy to get girls to work out in the country these days and Marta sees that everything runs smoothly without causing unrest among them. Unless,' she suggested as an afterthought, 'you have a complaint?'

'None at all where Marta's competence is concerned,' Eduardo told her, and Lari felt there was only one way to interpret that.

'Then it must be because you think I ought to know more about what goes on,' she guessed. 'It really isn't necessary, Eduardo. When my mother died I was too young to take any part in running the house and it just naturally evolved that Marta did it all.'

'That was reasonable in the circumstances,' Eduardo allowed, but Lari felt his dark and oddly disturbing gaze on her and stirred uneasily, wondering what to expect. 'But you're not a little girl now, Lari, you said so yourself, and you really should take charge of running the house, not leave it to the housekeeper, however experienced and efficient she might be. Marta must be more than seventy years old and she can't go on for ever; it's unlikely that the next housekeeper we have will be prepared to take on responsibilities that should be my wife's.'

Lari was tempted to remind him of the hollowness

of the title, but she resisted the temptation because she did not particularly want to start their first day of married life by quarrelling with him. Even though it looked as if things were drifting in that direction. 'Are you trying to say that I should take over from Marta?' she asked, unable to believe it.

'I'm saying that you should make yourself responsible for the things that the woman of the house normally does, that's all,' Eduardo told her. 'Things like supervising the amount of food that's bought, and choosing what we have to eat each day. The ordinary kind of things a wife does.'

'But I'm not an ordinary kind of wife, am I?' Lari asked, unable to resist some kind of retort even though she still clung to her vow not to quarrel with him.

'You understand me well enough, Lari,' he said firmly. 'And you can certainly manage simple housekeeping. I appreciate that it will be difficult starting at the beginning, but it needs only common sense and Marta's help, and I know she'll be willing to help. I'm quite sure you're bright enough to learn quickly.'

'Oh, I'm sure I am,' Lari agreed with deceptive mildness, and felt a moment of regret to see her good intentions go flying out of the window. 'I'm also bright enough to resent being treated like a schoolgirl who's getting an imposition for being naughty!'

'Indeed?'

There was something in the way his dark eyes regarded her that made her heart beat furiously hard and fast, and she put down the coffee pot before it betrayed the fact that her hands were shaking. 'You just won't admit that I've grown up, will you, Eduardo? I imagine you feel I should be grateful to you for marrying me and making it possible for me to stay on at Anchoterrias; just carrying on as I've always done?' she suggested, and somehow managed to steady her voice. But as I see it, Eduardo, *you're* the one with most to gain, and I have no intention of playing the meek little wife while you lord it over me, demanding blind obedience! I'm sorry, but if that's what you have in mind you're going to be very disappointed! Nor is that what Papá had in mind when he made that—that stupid will, either!'

'Have you quite finished?' His calmness was very probably a front, the look in his eyes suggested it was, but just the same it served to show up her determined bellicosity in the worst possible light, and she didn't answer him. 'What my uncle had in mind,' he went on when she made no reply, 'was for me to marry you and continue to care for you as he has done, and since I have every intention of carrying out his wishes to the letter, I can't understand your attitude at all. I undertake to see that you live exactly as you did when he was alive, so is it unreasonable of me to ask that in return you behave as a marrried woman should and take on the responsibility of running our home?'

Obviously he meant it to be all very cut and dried, with no emotions involved, and only those chaste kisses night and morning. It was the kind of prospect that Lari's warm and affectionate nature faced with abhorrence, and she found it hard to disguise the fact. 'I don't believe you have the remotest idea what Papá wanted,' she told him. 'And what *you* want is simply a well-trained replacement for when Marta retires!'

'Lari, stop it, you're talking nonsense!'

'And please don't try playing the heavy-handed husband,' she interrupted swiftly, 'it won't work, Eduardo, not with me!'

Eduardo made an impatient sound with his tongue and frowned. 'Now you're being completely unreasonable,' he decreed. 'Eat your breakfast and we'll try and bring some rational thinking to this before it gets out of hand!'

'Which is another way of saying you think you can

get your own way, given time,' Lari guessed, giving reason a nudge and allowing herself the privilege of being perverse. 'I'm sorry, Eduardo, I'm suddenly not hungry, and if you'll excuse me I've other things to do!'

'Lari, sit down!'

His voice rasped harshly with anger, and something in Lari reacted in a way she would not have believed possible. She did as he said, even though she sat with her hands pressed firmly around the coffee pot and looked flushed and defiant; glaring across at him with eyes that were so darkened by emotion they almost lost their blue colour and appeared nearly as black as his.

'Please—eat some breakfast, Lari.' The change in his voice took her unaware, and its soft deep tone slid along her spine like a caressing hand, making her shiver involuntarily. A faint smile hovered around his mouth, but the mouth itself was still slightly compressed, as if he contained his impatience only with difficulty. 'I concede that I was probably too hasty, I should have left you to find your own way to it. But I mean what I say, Lari.' He stretched out a hand and raised her chin with one finger, looking down at her mouth with a steady intensity that she found disturbing in the circumstances. 'Hmm?' he demanded softly, and she briefly lowered her eyelids in a gesture of agreement.

Silence followed while they finished their meal, and when Eduardo finished his and got to his feet with a murmured excuse, Lari looked up at him with eyes that reproached him for another of those light, cool kisses on her cheek. How different it was from what she had always imagined, she thought as she watched him go; how different, surely, from what her stepfather had imagined too. And yet she saw little hope of the situation changing unless she did something to change it, and at the moment she did not have quite enough confidence to try that.

CHAPTER THREE

WHILE her stepfather was alive Lari had spent all her time with him, for José Sagrera had been a sick and lonely old man who expected, without demanding, her full attention, and as a consequence she had made few friends. After his death and her own stay in hospital as a result of the accident in which he died, she had been a solitary figure, not quite sure of either her future or her own feelings.

In a way her marriage to Eduardo had set her free. Certainly it had freed her from the uncertainty of not knowing where she stood with regard to remaining at Anchoterrias, and it had also given her more confidence than she had had before. In the short time since, she had made a couple of trips to Seville for personal shopping, which was something she had seldom been able to do in her stepfather's time.

As a result Eduardo's wishes concerning her domestic duties had been pushed to the back of her mind and she frowned her dislike when he raised the matter one morning at breakfast, after hearing about her previous day's trip to Seville. 'Don't you approve of me going shopping?' she asked, knowing full well he had no such objection, and Eduardo sent her a long, meaningful look.

'You can go shopping as often as you want to,' he told her, 'but surely you can fit in a little attention to housekeeping too. Have you even mentioned it to Marta yet?' Lari shook her head and he pursed a disapproving lower lip. 'Then don't you think it's time you did, Lari?'

'If you say so.'

Eduardo put down his knife and rested his folded arms on the table, looking across at her steadily for a moment before he spoke. 'Are you thinking of staging a rebellion?' he enquired soft-voiced, and something in his tone brought swift colour to her cheeks. 'If you are, I wouldn't advise it.'

Her eyes widened and Lari tried to still the strange fluttering sensation that was neither fear nor excitement but a curious mingling of both. 'Are you threatening me?' she asked, and he reached over to draw one long finger across the soft flesh of her throat while he watched her with gleaming dark eyes.

'I know a time when I wouldn't have needed to,' he murmured. 'You were a very obedient child, Lari.'

'Only I'm no longer a child,' she reminded him.

Something in his eyes set her heart racing uncontrollably and she hastily avoided them. 'I still find it hard to remember it, Lari, and it's still true that I'm a good many years older than you are and, I venture to suggest, a good deal more experienced. Whether or not you realise it, Marta's getting on in years and is due for retirement very soon. Naturally I shall see that she's comfortable and doesn't want for anything; she deserves it after all the years she's looked after the Sagrera family.' Lari looked up swiftly, noting the way his eyes gleamed, leaving her in no doubt of his meaning. 'I would,' he promised, in reply to her unspoken question. 'So eat your breakfast, then go and take advantage of Marta's expertise while you still have the chance.'

This threat to retire Marta angered her, but it also made her fearful too, for Marta was a familiar and kindly figure from her childhood, and she would be lost without her as Eduardo must be well aware. Lari gulped down half her coffee in one breathtaking mouthful, then banged her empty cup down in the saucer. 'I haven't time for breakfast,' she gasped, scrambling to her feet. 'Marta goes to market this morning and if I'm to go with her I'd better hurry! Please excuse me!'

'Sit down, Lari, and stop being childish, for heaven's sake!'

Eduardo's voice was quiet, but something in its timbre roughened to match the gleaming hardness in his eyes and the tight firm look of his mouth. A different tone might have persuaded her, but the voice of authority and the reference to childishness put her on the defensive. 'No,' she insisted, 'I don't have time!'

Lari had the advantage of already being on her feet, and by the time Eduardo got up from his chair she was half-way across the *patio* and almost running in her determination to get away from him. He cursed under his breath and she heard the scrape of chair legs on the *patio* stones, but he didn't come after her, and that in itself she found hard to accept.

Obviously he didn't care enough to follow up a demand when she had deliberately flouted him, and she hated him with unexpected fury as she hurriedly left the sunlight for the shadowy coolness of the house. Nothing was working out as she wanted it to, and it was no consolation at all to have to admit that she was almost as much to blame for the present contretemps as Eduardo was.

As she anticipated, Marta was on the point of leaving for the village market in San Pedro, and seeing Lari come hurrying in, flushed and angry-eyed, she looked at her enquiringly. Casting a swift glance at the open door, she allowed herself a brief elevation of her thick black brows, but that was all.

'Is there something I can get for you, *señora*?' she enquired, and Lari noted with what relish she used the newly acquired title; Marta had always admired Eduardo, and considered any woman who married him to be very fortunate.

Lari was briefly at a loss, for Marta had known her

since she was a little girl and was fond of her, but there was no knowing how she would feel about handing over some of the authority that had been hers for so long. Required to find an answer, Lari plunged in quickly before she lost her nerve.

'I'm coming to market with you, Marta; we'll go by car.'

Marta evidently didn't quite grasp her meaning right away; when she did she eyed Lari narrowly, her black brows beetling. 'You want to come to market with me, *señorita—señora*?'

'That's right.' Lari resisted the temptation to tell her that it was Eduardo who was responsible for the decision, and hurried on. 'It seems it's time I took a hand in the running of the house and learned something about shopping and housekeeping, so just give me a minute to change my shoes and I'll be with you. Ask Pepe to bring the car round for me, will you?'

Marta had never liked riding in cars. Mostly she preferred her own two feet as her only means of transport, but very occasionally she would make a concession to her advancing years and accepted a lift on the back of someone's mule if it was offered. Cars she disliked, and Marta was privileged enough in her seniority to express her preference.

'If you'll forgive me, I prefer to walk, *señora,*' she stated categorically. 'But I'll ask Pepe to bring your car round for you.'

Knowing how adamant she was likely to be, Lari hesitated, and it was perhaps with the idea of making the most of the situation that she acted as she did. There was no harm in letting Eduardo see what his insistence had led to, and he might even suffer a qualm of conscience, although it was unlikely.

'Very well, I'll walk too,' she told an obviously startled Marta. 'If I'm to learn to be a good housekeeper

I'd better learn to be more energetic, and if it means walking to market, then I'll walk!'

'*You*'re to be housekeeper?'

Lari got a certain satisfaction from Marta's obvious astonishment as she nodded agreement. 'So my husband says. Apparently he's concerned that you do too much, Marta, and I'm to take over what he says are the things that every married woman does. He's looking to you to train me in the way I should go!'

'Ah!' Lari saw the ally she had counted on slipping away to the opposition when realisation dawned, and Marta's black eyes gleamed with barely suppressed mischief. 'There is no need to walk to San Pedro to learn what you have to learn, little *señora*,' she told her with the gentle understanding that Lari had counted on for so long. 'Señor Eduardo wouldn't like you doing that, and it isn't necessary.'

'You obviously don't know Señor Eduardo as well as you think you do!' Lari informed her. 'I assure you that in his present mood he'll think a long hot walk to San Pedro and back will be very good for my character!' She was already part way upstairs, and she paused and looked down at Marta's wrinkled face and watching black eyes. 'And if you go and tell him what I mean to do,' she insisted, 'you'll see how right I am!'

There was a sly, mischievous look on the older woman's face and her thin lips stretched into a smile for a moment while she shook her head slowly. 'If you think that,' she told her, '*you* don't know him at all, little *señora*!'

Lari had never had quite the same view of the countryside before, and the experience was novel enough in the beginning to take her mind off the unaccustomed hardship of trudging down a rough, dusty road that seemed far longer than it did when she drove down it in a car. Looking back she could see Anchoterrias sitting amid its acres of vines, a white dot on the fertile hillside, with the silver scribble of irrigation channels weaving in and out of the rows and catching the sun in fluctuating flashes of light.

Ahead the road sloped downward into San Pedro and to their left the valley spread out in the sun on a more gentle incline, patched with the dark and light of olives and grapes. Above it all and beyond the fertility of Anchoterrias soared the stark bare tops of the hills baked in the Andalusian sun, and it was hard to believe that the water used for irrigating the *viñas* came from those same hills. Spain was a country of contrasts, and none more so than the province of Andalusia.

Accustomed as she was to the Spanish sun, Lari was not used to walking the distance into the village, and particularly not when she was wearing shoes that were not made for rough country roads. Marta was shod in thick black shoes that clopped firmly at every step and sent up little puffs of dust, and she had the steady, plodding tread of the habitual walker despite her age, so that Lari almost envied her.

Half way down the hill a small shrine stood at the roadside, decked with flowers that had already wilted in the sun, and from the way Marta turned aside and knelt for a moment on the worn steps, it was obvious that her brief act of devotion was habitual and quite automatic. She looked as aged and as ageless as the countryside around her, and Lari wondered at the stamina required of a woman of seventy to make this same journey twice each week and twice on Sundays.

Approaching San Pedro on foot was different too, for there was time to notice the little houses and shops, instead of passing them by in a flash. The modern supermarket as such had so far bypassed San Pedro and the old-fashioned open market stalls had their wares spread out under striped awnings, a mingling of scents in the hot air. Every conceivable type of fish, fruit and vegetable was offered for sale.

Produce in abundance was there to be inspected and mulled over before purchase, and Lari gained a completely new insight into housekeeping. Even so the novelty began to pall after a while, and while she stood listening to Marta make yet another complaint about prices, she wished she had been less impulsive; less anxious to put Eduardo in the wrong.

Her feelings were evidently more obvious than she realised, for when Marta turned from making her latest purchase she looked at her knowingly, and a hint of smile lurked in her eyes. 'The walk has tired you, *señora,*' she suggested. 'Why don't you call on Señor Eduardo's sister for a while? I'm quite sure Señora Morenas would welcome a visit from you.'

Lari was equally sure that her newly acquired sister-in-law would be less welcoming than Marta anticipated, but she refrained from saying so. Instead she made a decision on the spur of the moment, following an inclination she had had in mind ever since the wedding reception.

'I've got a better idea,' she said. 'Rather than go calling unexpectedly, I'll see if I can get a copy of Eric Truman's book. He's the writer who lives right next to us, who was at the wedding, do you remember I told you?'

'I remember, *señora,*' said Marta, her opinion in no doubt, 'and I'm sure Señor Eduardo wouldn't like that book brought into the house. It's fit only for the trash can. Father Ortega says, and Señor Eduardo wouldn't like you reading it, *señora!*'

'Then he'll have to put up with it!' Lari retorted, in arms at the idea of Eduardo daring to censor her reading matter. 'You'll know where to find me when you're ready to leave, Marta.'

'I'm almost ready now, *señora.*'

Lari smiled to herself; Marta never gave up easily. 'Then you go and finish what you have to do and I'll get my book,' she told her, frustrating any further attempt to stop her by walking off quickly in the direction of the newsagents.

In fact she felt a little mean for being so sharp with Marta, but she felt she had to assert her independence, and show them that she meant what she said about not being blindly obedient. Eduardo himself had pointed out that she was no longer a little girl, and that surely implied that she was woman enough to dictate her own actions.

Wrapped in her thoughts, she walked on heedlessly, and she was turning a corner when she collided quite forcibily with someone coming from the other direction. Automatically she put out a hand to save herself and found herself face to face with the very man whose book she was on her way to buy.

Eric Truman took her hand in both of his and held it tightly while those disarmingly smiling grey eyes watched her face and noted the sudden warm colour in her cheeks. Raising her hand to his lips, he kissed her fingers lightly, not once moving his eyes from her face. 'This *is* an unexpected pleasure, Señora Sagrera!'

It was quite instinctive when Lari glanced hastily over her shoulder, for Marta wasn't likely to have followed her. 'I'm sorry,' she apologised, 'I wasn't looking where I was going.'

'Daydreaming?' Eric Truman suggested, and somehow managed to suggest that he might have been the subject of her dreams.

'Actually I was on my way to the bookshop,' Lari told him, and the grey eyes glowed even more warmly, his hand still holding hers.

'To buy my book?' he suggested, and when she nodded looked quite inordinately pleased. 'You *were*? But there's really no need to buy it, my dear *señora*;

I'll be delighted to present you with a signed copy!'

It was difficult to meet his eyes without feeling a glow of self-satisfaction, for such open admiration was very good for her ego. 'You're very kind,' she murmured, but he waved her thanks aside.

'On the contrary,' he disagreed blandly, 'I want to have you in my debt!' A sudden burst of laughter turned what could have been an embarrassing statement into a joke, yet something in the way he looked when he said it gave Lari the impression that he had been perfectly serious about putting her in his debt. Making exaggerated checks to ensure she was alone, he raised a brow. 'No one with you?'

Lari was tempted to find out what he would suggest if he thought she was alone, but thought better of it. 'At the moment,' she agreed, 'but Marta isn't far away. Our housekeeper; I left her to finish the shopping while I went to the bookshop.'

'Oh, I see, you're chaperoned.'

There was something in the way he said it that made her colour furiously, but Lari shook her head and made a real effort at last to free her hand. 'No, Señor Truman, I'm not chaperoned. Marta and I walked down to do the shopping, that's all.'

'Walked?' He was staring at her in disbelief, and it was a moment or two before Lari realised the reason for his expression of shock. 'Good God,' he said, 'that new husband of yours doesn't really make you walk all that way to do the shopping, does he? Haven't you got a car? A chauffeur?'

'Oh yes, of course I have my own car.' Lari hastened to correct the impression she had given. 'I just chose to walk with Marta, but it isn't a thing I always do; as a matter of fact I never have before today.'

It was obvious that he found it hard to believe, even now, and he was shaking his head over it. 'Well, at least let me buy you a drink while your housekeeper finishes the shopping,' he suggested. 'And then I'll run you home and save you the walk back. And your housekeeper, of course,' he added as an obviously unenthusiastic afterthought.

There was no reason why she shouldn't have a drink with a fellow countryman, Lari told herself, and was still trying to convince herself when she saw Marta turn the corner and narrow her sharp black eyes at the sight of her with Eric Truman. '*Señora?*' her gentle enquiry from a discreet distance also carried a warning, but Lari chose to ignore it.

'We're riding back with Señor Truman, Marta,' she told her, in Spanish because Marta had no English to speak of, and the old woman's expression was opinion enough.

'I prefer not, *señora.*'

It wasn't strictly speaking a refusal, merely a statement of her personal feelings, but it amounted to the same thing in the end, and Lari was taking a deep breath to try and persuade her when Eric Truman took a hand. Marta's face had a stubborn passivity that told its own story and he must have realised what was going on even though he couldn't understand their Spanish.

'If you want to walk, you walk,' he told Marta, and there was a hard determined look about his mouth, 'but Señora Sagrera's had enough walking, and she's driving back with me!'

It was doubtful if Marta understood even half of what he said, but the gist of it was plain enough and she glared at him indignantly when he held out a hand for the basket she carried. She hesitated a moment, then handed it over, murmuring something under her breath. And when Lari watched her trudge off alone a few moments later, she felt sure the old lady would stop again at the little shrine and murmur an *Ave* for the good of Lari's soul, and for her swift enlightenment.

'Now your watchdog has been disposed of, shall we go and have that drink?'

The persuasive voice spoke close to her ear and Lari turned, smiling a little uncertainly, for she was already having doubts about the wisdom of what she was doing. Yet she was hardly a bride in the accepted sense of the word and there was something very tempting in the grey eyes that looked at her so invitingly.

'Just one,' she said, 'and then I must go home.'

It was much later than she had intended when Lari made her way across the *patio*, only vaguely aware of the sound of Eric Truman's car gradually receding along the dusty track through the vineyards, and she had already made up her mind to tell Eduardo where she had been. It would probably have been as well to clean up and brush her hair first, but it seemed imperative to tell him if she was going to, and get it over with.

Marta might almost have been lying in wait for her, for she emerged from the kitchen the moment Lari came into the house, and took the basket from her. There was an oddly disturbing look in her eyes, but for the moment Lari was intent on making a clean breast of her interlude with Eric Truman and she ignored everything else.

'Is Señor Eduardo in the *salón*?' she asked, already making her way across there, and Marta called after her.

'Yes, *señora*, but he's——'

The hint of warning came just too late, for Lari opened the door of the *salón* at exactly the same moment as Juana Cortez stood on tiptoe and kissed Eduardo firmly and passionately full on his mouth. Neither of them was aware of her until the moment her breath caught audibly in her throat, then Eduardo turned at once, and she saw his look of blank dismay.

Just as obvious was the bright challenging gleam in Juana Cortez's dark eyes and Lari turned quickly, blindly seeking to efface herself.

'Lari!'

She cut off Eduardo's cry when she slammed the *salón* door behind her, but even so she heard the low murmur of Juana Cortez's voice, soothing and persuasive, and her legs were shaking so much she did not know how she managed to walk across the hall. She had reached the foot of the stairs when Eduardo came hurrying out into the hall, and it was anger, she told herself, that made her brush a hasty hand across her eyes to clear the tears from them.

Why should she cry over a man who had married her simply for the purpose of inheriting his uncle's estate, and made no excuse for it? He had never pretended any other feeling than a mild affection for her and he would probably have married Juana Cortez instead if she could have brought him Anchoterrias.

'Lari, wait a moment, please! Don't be misled by what you thought you saw!'

'Oh, I know what I saw!' Standing on the second step up, Lari turned to face him and found herself in the unusual position of being able to look him in the eye for once. Her voice shivered a little, but she controlled it remarkably well in the circumstances. 'But please don't let me disturb you, Eduardo! I'm fully aware that being married to me involves none of the usual emotions and—and loyalties; it was merely a necessary evil to achieve what you wanted!' Her right hand gripped the newel post tightly, yet she still managed to remain outwardly calm, or so she hoped. 'I'm just sorry I came in at an inopportune moment, and I hope Señora Cortez isn't too embarrassed.'

'Stop it, Lari!' She caught her breath when long hard fingers closed over her hand and pressed it over the post until she flinched from the pain it caused her, and his eyes were very hard to meet. 'What you saw in there was——'

'I'm really not interested!' Lari insisted. 'You don't have to account to me for your actions, Eduardo, any more than I have to account to you. Although as a matter of fact,' she went on in reckless haste, 'I was coming in to tell you that I've been gone so long because I saw Eric Truman in the village and we had a drink together before he drove me home. Not that it matters to you, of course, but I don't suppose people know what the situation is with us and if someone saw me with him and——' She shrugged with apparent carelessness. 'Well, you know what people are for gossip, and it might have been passed on to you.'

Evidently he knew nothing about her trip to San Pedro, he probably thought she had been bluffing when she said she was going with Marta, and the sudden darkening of his eyes was a warning she couldn't ignore. 'You've seen the Englishman again?'

'Oh, I didn't go with the intention of meeting him,' she denied, 'I'm not *that* deceitful.' Glancing at the *salón* door he had closed so carefully behind him left her meaning in no doubt. 'In the circumstances it's probably as well I decided to walk down with Marta.'

Contrary to expectations Eduardo didn't take up the implication concerning his visitor, but seemed more impressed by the rest of her statement. 'You *walked* to San Pedro?'

'After our conversation at breakfast, I thought a little hard physical exercise would meet with your approval!'

'You little idiot!'

His voice deepened, bringing a clamouring response from every nerve in her body. In the past few days it had startled her to realise that it was during their moments of disagreement that Eduardo stirred her most deeply, when mild tolerance gave way to more passionate emotions; and defying him was irresistible.

'Aren't you grateful that I left you free of possible interruptions for a couple of hours?' she demanded in a slightly unsteady voice. 'If you'd said you were having your—mother's cousin's son's widow?—here, I'd have co-operated quite willingly. Why not? I don't mind.'

'You *dare*!' His fury blazed at her from glittering dark eyes, and the bruisingly hard press of his hand on hers tightened even more until she struggled to free it. He let go her hand and grasped her wrist instead, pulling her down the two steps she had mounted, and forcing her close to the lean angry length of him, a contact that made her shiver with more than anxiety. 'You dare to suggest that I'd bring another woman here——'

'Why not?' Lari demanded desperately, her emotions too tangled to be easily identified. 'It's a reasonable assumption in the circumstances!'

'You wouldn't recognise reason if you saw it!' Eduardo declared harshly. 'If you weren't so stubbornly shortsighted you'd know you're talking nonsense—insulting nonsense at that!' He heaved a great sigh, making an effort to bring his formidable temper under control again. 'But this isn't the time or the place to go into it; Juana is waiting in the *salón*, and you should come and welcome her as our first caller. Don't give her the wrong impression, Lari—come on!'

In view of what she had just witnessed between them Lari found it hard to believe that he actually expected her to act the polite hostess to that sleekly handsome woman in there, and she stared at him for a moment in silence. Her eyes were so dark that their blue colour appeared to be almost black, and she held tightly to the balustrade with her free hand.

'I'm sure you'll understand when I say I'd rather not,' she said in a small voice. 'I'm broadminded, I hope, and I'd be the first to allow that our marriage has nothing to do with love or romance, but there are limits, Eduardo!' She went on, ignoring the growing storm in his eyes that sent little thrills of an unfamiliar emotion fluttering along her spine. 'Oh, it has nothing to do with jealousy, of course, only my pride; that's something I'm sure you'll understand, although you probably think it's the sole prerogative of the Spanish male!'

'You——' Eduardo drew in a long slow breath and let it out again, obviously exerting remarkable self-control. 'Very well, go to your room, if that's what you want to do!' he told her harshly. 'I'll try and make sense of you when you're in a more reasonable frame of mind, but in the meantime do me the favour of staying out of my way! I don't trust myself not to give you what you deserve, and I have to keep in mind the conditions of Tío José's will!'

She snatched at her captive arm, and this time he let her go, watching as she hastily put several steps between them before she turned and delivered a parting shot. 'Why should you bother now?' she demanded. 'You've got what you want!'

'Lari!'

She turned again swiftly and raced up the wide staircase with his voice following her. Hurrying along the galleried landing, she went into her room and closed the door, standing with her back against it for a moment or two listening. But no one came after her, so presumably Eduardo had returned to his guest, and Lari wished it didn't hurt quite so much to remember him with Juana Cortez in his arms. How often, she wondered, must she remind herself that theirs was a marriage of convenience?

If Lari could have avoided joining Eduardo for lunch, she would have done; as it was she delayed as long as possible and consequently it was much later than usual when she put in an appearance. The long, low-ceilinged dining *salón* was one of her favourite rooms with its shuttered windows open to the *patio* and heavy dark furniture contrasted with plain white walls. A quiet restful room.

Eduardo got up from a seat by the window when she came in and she noticed him look very pointedly at his wrist-watch. 'I'd almost given you up,' he said. 'It's three o'clock.'

Lari took her seat at the table, almost flinching from the proximity of him when he pushed in her chair, and instead of looking to start a conversation as she was seated as they usually did, she took a bread roll from the basket and crumbled it in restless hands. 'You should have started without me,' she told him. 'I'm not very hungry.'

'Well, you should be,' Eduardo declared firmly. 'You're young and healthy and you've walked a long way this morning.' His dark eyes sought and held hers determinedly. 'And if you're hoping to make me feel conscience-stricken, Lari, you're going to be disappointed! Juana was here because she happens to be staying with the family at Santa Inés and, naturally, she came over to see us.'

'To see *you*,' Lari argued insistently. 'You can't seriously suggest she'd come to see me, Eduardo.'

Something in the dark depths of his eyes stirred strange responses in her, and a faint smile hovered about his mouth. 'Are you jealous, Lari?' he asked softly.

It was too close to the truth for comfort and consequently she denied it swiftly and adamantly. 'Good heavens, no! Why should I be? I'm not in the same position as most brides, after all.'

What was the use of building up false hopes? Juana Cortez seemed to have haunted her ever since their wedding day and she was not a woman to give up easily. She had done little to disguise her feelings for

Eduardo and she was obviously a very determined lady. But there was a look in his eyes at the moment that sent tiny shivers slithering along her spine like the touch of icy fingertips.

'And she's not really your cousin, is she?' she pressed, in a small breathless voice, and watched his eyes narrow as they moved slowly over her flushed face.

'You think she's my lover?' he asked quietly, and Lari caught her breath. If she was, she realised suddenly, she didn't want to hear him say so, and she passed the tip of her tongue over her dry lips.

How she would have answered, he never found out, for Marta's appearance with a huge dish of her special paella put a stop to conversation for several minutes. And it was a curious fact that when her plate was filled with the spicy mixture of rice, prawns and chicken Lari's appetite seemed to return and she gave her attention to satisfying a normally healthy hunger.

For several minutes they ate their meal in silence; only the birds out in the *patio* garden breaking the hot stillness with their fluting whistles. Of the two of them Eduardo seemed the more relaxed, but his cool air of detachment, Lari knew only too well, could be no more than a front.

Marta, in her wisdom, had set both places at the same end of the long table, so that it was impossible to go on ignoring one another for very long. Lari would willingly have been the one to make peace, but hard as she tried, that brief sight of Juana Cortez in Eduardo's arms would not be dismissed, and while it continued to trouble her she feared that the intimacy his nearness suggested could never become a fact.

Picking up the bottle of wine to refill his glass, Eduardo looked at the label, then cocked a questioning brow at her. 'Did you choose the wine?' he asked, and Lari shook her head.

'No, Marta did.' She scooped up another forkful of

rice and prawns and popped it into her mouth, savouring it for a second or two before she went on. 'I thought you realised, Eduardo; I haven't begun my housekeeping course yet.'

When she reached for her wine glass Eduardo placed a large and so far gentle hand over hers, and she looked up warily. 'Let it rest, Lari, please! I was merely going to say that it's a very good wine and suggest, hopefully, that we forget what happened this morning and start afresh; do you agree?'

Lari used her fork to bury a piece of chicken in saffron-coloured rice and didn't answer at once. Not because she was unwilling to do as he said, but because she did not quite see how it was going to be possible. His attitude towards her knowing Eric Truman hardly suggested tolerance in that direction, and there was still the matter of Juana Cortez, sleek and sophisticated and much nearer his age.

'Lari?'

The deep soft voice and the slight pressure of his fingers on her hand were irresistible, and she nodded. 'All right,' she agreed. 'If you really think it will work.'

'We'll *make* it work!' His long fingers moved caressingly back and forth over the soft skin of her inner wrist and the effect of it was startlingly evocative, making her tremble. 'Beginning now,' he decided, and leaned across the corner of the table to kiss her cheek. Lari's senses rebelled at the chaste coolness of it as they always did and as if he sensed how she felt, he brushed her lips with the warm firmness of his mouth. 'And please stop looking as if you expect me to do something unspeakable to you, Lari, eh?'

It was so hard to resist that deep glowing darkness in his eyes, so she allowed herself to be lured by their warmth, and nodded. 'I'd rather be friends,' she murmured, and didn't notice the swift drawing of his black brows for a moment before he replied.

'Friends,' he agreed, and kissed her cheek lightly again.

If Lari realised how tenuous their truce was, she thrust it firmly to the back of her mind and accepted that at least during the last couple of days Eduardo had approved of her efforts to learn from Marta's vast experience of housekeeping. It was some satisfaction too that those coolly chaste kisses had quite definitely developed a deeper and more lingering warmth, and she was feeling much more relaxed and happy when she drove her car into the garage in San Pedro for a minor adjustment to the engine.

The proprietor was busy in his tiny workshop with another customer when she drove in, and she didn't recognise the man with him until he called out to her, 'Good morning, Señora Sagrera!'

Lari let down the car window and smiled at Eric Truman a little uncertainly. She could hardly ignore him, and yet she felt she would much rather not have seen him now that things were going so promisingly with Eduardo. 'Señor Truman.'

The proprietor stood by, polite but nevertheless interested, but it was doubtful if Eric Truman even realised his interest, he was too intent on charming Lari. With an arm along the roof of her car he leaned down to speak to her. 'This is an unexpected pleasure,' he told her, and his study of her face was more Latin than English in its boldness. 'It's also very lucky,' he went on. 'My car's decided to pack up on me and I'm wondering if I can prevail on you to give me a lift home; can I?'

She had to agree, Lari realised, and those smiling grey eyes suggested he had little doubt she would. 'Yes, of course,' she said. 'I have to get something done to my engine first, but it won't take many minutes.'

'Señora?'

The man was well known to both her and Eduardo and there was a speculative glint in his eyes as he came forward, as if he was weighing up the situation. She gave him a brief explanation of what was wrong, and he lifted the bonnet, burying half his torso under it for several minutes, during which time Eric Truman looked at her and smiled. It was a curiously intimate smile that made her uneasy so that she hastily looked away, but she knew he still watched her; trying to judge her reaction, she guessed.

'Is this likely to take long?' he asked, and Lari steeled herself against the inevitable follow-on. The garage man glanced up for a moment, then shrugged without committing himself. 'Long enough for us to have a drink, I'm sure,' Eric went on. 'Do you agree, *señora?*'

'Oh no, *señor*, thank you!'

She saw from the corner of her eye the mechanic glance up for a moment, and rued the warm flush of colour in her cheeks as much as she did her own temptation to accept. 'Why not?' Eric insisted. 'It's bound to take time to fix whatever it is, and it won't take long to have a drink.'

'There, that should hold it, *señora*!' The man spoke to her in Spanish and Eric therefore wasn't sure what he'd said.

Frowning, he looked at him suspiciously until the mechanic banged down the bonnet, than he made a sharp *tch* of impatience. 'Oh damn!' he swore, openly disappointed, then looked at Lari again with that half bold, half appealing look that was so difficult to resist. 'We could still go for that drink,' he told her.

'No, thanks, *señor*!'

Lari was anxious to get away. There was no way she could avoid driving him home, but she wanted to do so as quickly as possible, before she was talked into something she knew she would be sorry for. Turning to the proprietor she thanked him and reminded him to put the repair on to Eduardo's bill, then she paused in the act of getting into the car and looked at Eric enquiringly.

'You do still want me to drive you home, *Señor* Truman?'

Clearly he didn't like the way she had so definitely refused him, but apparently he was prepared to make the best of it, and with a rueful smile he climbed into the car beside her. 'Half a loaf,' he murmured as he got in, and Lari looked at him curiously.

'*Señor?*'

There was a faint glitter in his eyes when he turned his head, and she thought he was even more annoyed than she had realised. 'You *have* been away from home a long time, haven't you?' he asked. 'It's an old English saying, Señora Sagrera, when one has to make the best of a situation. Half a loaf is better than no bread at all; have you never heard it?'

'Never.'

She had the uneasy feeling that he was being mildly funny at her expense, but she did not propose to press for further enlightenment, and she started up the car. The engine still did not sound quite as it should, but at least it got them out of San Pedro and on to the valley road that swept steeply upward towards Anchoterrias.

It was impossible to ignore the fact that she was under observation while she was driving, and Lari was aware that the dress she wore flattered and stressed her softly rounded figure. Eric Truman took explicit note of it all the time they were driving up the steep dusty road above the valley. She had seldom driven with anyone but her stepfather in the passenger seat beside her, and the proximity of her present passenger was the more disturbing because of it.

'What made them call you Lari?' His hand on her arm made her grip the steering wheel in sudden anxiety to avoid a swerve. 'It isn't very English, is it?'

'It's short for Larissa,' Lari explained, hastily recovering herself. 'My parents spent their honeymoon in Greece and they liked the name.'

'You're much prettier than the place,' he told her, and obviously expected her to comment on the fact that he had been there.

Instead she kept quiet and thanked heaven that they were approaching the access to his property. The house was built much nearer to the public road than Anchoterrias was, and had less vegetation surrounding it, so that it was easy to see that he could have quite easily seen her drive by with her stepfather sometimes, as he said. Whatever he expected, it was clearly not to be dropped at the public end of the access road, and he half turned in his seat to face her.

'Won't you come in for a few minutes?' he asked, and Lari shook her head.

'No, thank you, *señor*. I'm glad to have been of help, but I won't stop, thank you.'

He hesitated, then climbed out of the car, but he was still reluctant to give up, and he leaned on one arm, looking in at her. His grey eyes again showed that glint of resentment, though he did his best to disguise it with a smile. 'I've heard of the girl who can't say no,' he remarked, 'but you're obviously the one who can't say anything else!'

'I'm sorry.'

His vehemence startled her and she sat facing the road, with a soft warm colour in her cheeks that must have told him his jibe had gone home. And after a second or two he sighed and shook his head. 'No, I'm sorry,' he insisted. 'And I do hope you won't refuse to see me again if the chance comes up. We will meet again, won't we, *señora*?'

'It's always possible, *señor*.'

He stood for a moment with one hand on the open

door and there was a curiously speculative look in his eyes. 'Will you tell your husband that you've seen me?' he asked, and Lari stared at him. He laughed, a short, harsh sound that was without a trace of humour. 'Silly question,' he decided, then heaved a sigh of resignation and straightened up. 'See you!'

He slammed the door and Lari drove off without turning her head or even waving a hand to him in parting. Eric Truman was the kind of disturbing character she could well do without, and she did not think she *would* tell Eduardo about him.

CHAPTER FOUR

LARI'S first thought when a bouquet of carnations arrived for her the following morning was that they had come from Eduardo, and she hugged the blooms to her breast delightedly, not yet noticing that Marta did not look as pleased as she might have expected her to be. They smelled so lovely and they were every one of them a pure snow white, so that they appeared both exotic and virginal.

'Oh, but they're gorgeous!' she said, and only then realised the expression on Marta's face. Inhaling the exotic perfume, she frowned at her curiously. 'Marta! Aren't you pleased that he's given me flowers? I can't imagine why he didn't give them to me himself, but—oh, it doesn't matter at all!'

'*Señora.*' Marta handed over the small gilt-edged card that must have come with them, and as Lari took it she experienced her first chill of doubt. 'It came with them, *señora,* and it wasn't in an envelope, so I couldn't help seeing what it said.'

'*Many thanks*', Lari read, and it was signed, '*Eric*'. Then followed a hastily scrawled postscript, and it was that as much as anything that brought the colour to her cheeks. '*You'll know why I sent pure white ones, won't you?*'

Even with a gesture of thanks he was mocking her insistence that she couldn't drink with him, and she wondered what Eduardo would have said to that. In fact she was less concerned with Eric Truman's opinion than with Eduardo's and she looked anxiously at the housekeeper. 'Marta, what shall I do?'

'Throw them away,' Marta advised without hesitation, and saw the way she looked at the thought of deliberately spoiling all those perfect blooms. 'It's much the best thing, *señora,*' she insisted. 'How would Señor Eduardo feel if he discovered that another man is sending flowers to his bride? You must get rid of them, *señora,* for his sake as well as for your own.'

'Yes. Yes, of course I must.' Lari looked at the carnations and tried to think of an alternative to destruction, but found none. Shaking her head, she handed them to Marta, but she had the most awful sense of guilt as she did so. 'Throw them away, Marta.' She re-read the accompanying card then thrust that at her too. 'And this,' she said. 'That most of all!'

Marta pushed the card into the pocket of her skirt. 'Yes, of course, *señora.*'

Lari felt suddenly much less lighthearted and Marta recognised it. Her black eyes pitied her, much more for her disappointment over the donor as for having to destroy flowers she was so fond of, and her sympathy did nothing to make Lari feel any better. 'Better be quick,' she told Marta, 'in case Eduardo comes in early for his morning break.'

Marta turned without a word and Lari heard her crossing the hall, but only seconds later she heard the sound of the outside door opening and Eduardo's voice, unmistakably enquiring. His actual words were indistinguishable, but her heart was thudding hard as she listened to Marta's equally indistinguishable reply.

There was no further conversation, but his footsteps came quickly across the hall, and she caught her breath when he came into the *salón* and stood for a moment looking across at her. 'It seems you have an unknown admirer,' he said, and although his voice sounded as deep and smooth as usual, Lari's senses were sufficiently alert to detect an edge of harshness too.

'Not—exactly unknown, Eduardo.' Heaven knew what had made her be so frank when she could easily have passed it off in the way Marta had obviously suggested. 'When I went to have my car attended to yesterday,' she went on in answer to a swiftly arched brow, 'I saw—I mean Eric Truman was there at the same time, only he had to leave his at the garage. I gave him a lift back; as a matter of fact he asked me if I would, and I couldn't very well say no.'

Eduardo's eyes were concealed by their thick lashes, and his voice was so quiet its resonance was lost in softness. 'Did you want to say no?'

Resentment stirred in her because she knew he suspected eagerness on her part to take up the request, and she lifted her chin in defiance of his opinion. 'I wasn't happy about agreeing,' she told him, 'because I know how much you dislike me having anything to do with him.'

'And you find that unreasonable of me, I suppose?'

'No, not unreasonable, just—unnecessary. I do know how to say no when it's necessary, Eduardo, but refusing to give a neighbour a lift when his car had broken down *would* have been unreasonable. The flowers you saw Marta taking away were what he sent as a gesture of thanks for helping out, that's all.'

'Marta told me that you asked for them to be destroyed,' he went on, and Lari wished he would let the matter rest. It was surely enough that she had told all there was to know about the incident, without his probing further.

'That's right,' she said, 'it seemed like the best thing to do in the circumstances.' She resumed the seat she had left when Marta brought in the carnations, and picked up the book she had been reading, giving it her attention rather than look at him. 'If you hadn't come in when you did, you'd never have known anything about them.'

'I see.'

The response was non-committal, and she looked up

at him briefly. 'I don't think you do,' she argued mildly. 'I wasn't being underhand for my own sake, Eduardo, but I guessed you wouldn't like the idea of him sending me flowers for whatever reason, and I thought it best to dispose of them before you knew anything about it.'

'And you've told me after all?'

Lari was puzzled herself by her reason for doing so and she sighed exaggeratedly while still flicking through the book she held. 'Because it seems I'm just not devious enough,' she told him, and went on without stopping to think. 'I sometimes think you'd have been much more in character adopting me instead of marrying me, Eduardo, for you're reacting far more like a disapproving parent than a husband! Even one whose only interest in me was to get possession of his inheritance!'

'Damn you, Lari!'

His vehemence startled her as he came striding over to her, and he snatched the book from her hands, flinging it into the chair beside her. Eyes glowing darkly, he hovered over her like a predator about to pounce and Lari shivered involuntarily, unsure what to expect. Her whole being yearned for the touch of him; for the gentle touch of his hands and the warm vigorous proximity of his body, and yet the only passion she seemed able to rouse in him was anger.

As if he exterted some powerful control over himself suddenly, he ran both hands through the thick blackness of his hair and shook his head slowly back and forth for a moment before he looked at her again. 'There's too much truth in what you say for me to deny it,' he said, and his quietness was in such direct contrast to his recent violence that she scarcely trusted it. 'I *did* marry you so that I could get Anchoterrias; what I didn't realise was——'

He sighed and sank into one of the armchairs with

his big hands clasped together between his knees. Then looking up suddenly his eyes scanned slowly over her face, and it was impossible for her to even guess what was going on behind them, dark and shadowed as they were.

'I always thought I knew you so well, Lari,' he said, and with such an air of uncertainty that her heart fluttered in response, dangerously close to tenderness. 'You were always such a—soft and gentle child, and so much in need of someone to look after you.'

'And you could wrap me around your little finger,' Lari acknowledged huskily.

'What happened to that girl, Lari?'

The softness of his voice was his most potent weapon, she decided dazedly. He could affect her more deeply than she felt was desirable in the circumstances, for the feeling she had for him now had little resemblance to the heady dreams of a fifteen-year-old, and she wished her youthful dreams had prepared her for a handicap like Juana Cortez.

Perhaps Eduardo was at last beginning to realise he had not married the young and easily manipulated girl he remembered. But she found it hard to believe he genuinely expected her to accept the fact of his lover without turning a hair, and if he did, he had a lot to learn.

'I grew up,' she told him. 'We all do, you know, Eduardo; I'm no exception, and six years is a long time.'

She avoided his eyes when they sought to hold hers, but it was less easy to escape the deep seduction of his voice and her senses responded as they always did. Leaning forward in his chair, he reached for her hand and long gentle fingers closed over hers with a slight pressure that in itself was a caress, setting her pulse racing hard again.

'Then it seems I shall have to learn to know you all

over again,' he suggested, and she glanced up at him for a moment.

'Do you really want to?' Lari asked huskily, and again the hard fingers exerted their gentle pressure.

'Oh yes, I'm quite sure I want to,' that irresistible voice assured her, and his mouth brushed lightly across her fingers. 'I think I must!'

When one of the maids announced a caller the following morning, the last person Lari expected was Juana Cortez. With Marta's assistance she was making out the week's menus, and she looked up and frowned when she heard who was calling, on edge even before she was shown in.

A deep blue velvet suit made the most of her tall slender figure, and Juana Cortez entered the *salón* rather as if she owned it. A pale cream blouse did wonders for her dark complexion, and high heels made her tower over Lari, whose light shoes added a bare half-inch to her height. Her black eyes took in the cosy domesticity of the scene and a smile hovered about her dark red mouth as if what she saw amused her.

Marta got up from her chair at once and seemed to hover just behind Lari almost defensively, something that also apparently amused the caller. 'I do hope I'm not interrupting anything important,' she drawled, looking from one to the other.

'Oh no, nothing very important,' Lari assured her, hoping her voice would not betray the way she felt. 'We're going through the week's menus, that's all. Please do sit down, Señora Cortez; how are you?'

The newcomer sank gracefully into one of the armchairs. 'You look very domesticated,' she remarked, her smile mocking. 'But do carry on, I can wait until you've finished.'

'If you're sure——' Lari was uneasy; unsure why she was there and suspicious of her motives. 'We only have one more item to settle and then we've finished.'

A generous hand conceded priority to their domestic arrangements, and once more that half-smile seemed to find amusement in it. 'Please!'

Lari looked upon it as a brief respite from having to make conversation with a woman whom she frankly disliked, and she once more took the list that Marta handed her, bringing her mind back to more mundane matters. 'Supper on Friday,' she mused aloud. 'Omelettes after the soup, I think, don't you? Mushroom and ham perhaps for Señor Eduardo, and—I'll have shrimps in mine. The new girl does know not to put mushrooms into anything for me, doesn't she, Marta?'

'Yes, *señora*, I've made very sure of that!'

Detecting interest, Lari glanced across at her caller and noticed an arched, enquiring brow. 'Don't you like mushrooms?' Juana asked. 'Or don't they agree with you?'

She sat back in her chair with one elegant leg crossed over the other, looking very much at ease and still smiling that oddly disturbing smile, but Lari found it hard to believe that she had any real interest in anything as commonplace as her appetite.

'It's something I'm almost ashamed to admit to,' Lari confessed, 'but I simply can't eat mushrooms. Something to do with certain acids or something, so I've been told; all I know is that one mushroom and I'm ill.'

'Really?' A fine black brow suggested disbelief rather than concern. 'Well, I'm glad you don't deprive Eduardo of them because you can't eat them, he's so *very* fond of mushrooms, I know.'

Her air of authority when she spoke of what Eduardo liked made Lari wonder just how familiar this woman was with his likes and dislikes, and her own reply was formed mostly in defiance of it. 'I learned that when I was quite small,' she claimed as she handed the list back to Marta. 'And speaking of eating. Señora Cortez, forgive me for not having offered you something. Coffee? Or perhaps a glass of wine?'

'Nothing, thank you.' From the way she glanced at Marta it was fairly clear that she was waiting for her to leave before she mentioned whatever it was she had come for. Lari's smile and nod seemed to comply with her wish, although in truth she had no wish to be alone with her. 'Your housekeeper guards you with her life!' The mocking suggestion followed Marta's closing the door, and Lari flushed.

'She very likely would if she thought it necessary, *señora*,' she told her. 'Marta's known me since I was a little girl and she cared for me when I was too young to look after myself. But are you sure I can't ask her to bring some coffee for us?'

'Quite sure, thank you. In fact I came to see Eduardo, although I should have known he wouldn't be here!'

Although she kept a firm control on her temper, Lari was fuming inwardly at the sheer insolence of the woman. 'No, you wouldn't find him here. As you say, at this hour of the day he's busy; Eduardo takes his role of owner very seriously.'

The next move was up to her visitor, Lari thought, and she sat with her hands clasped together on her lap. Outwardly she was cool under that hostile scrutiny, but inwardly she was seething and it took all the self-control she possessed to hide it. 'I wonder if he's mentioned it to you,' Juana Cortez said after a brief pause. 'He promised to find me another *capataz* and I'm anxious to know if he's had any luck. My last man left in a huff and I'm really no judge of what makes a man fit to put in charge of others, except on an executive level, of course. Since my husband died I'm afraid I've been very dependent on the wretched man and he tried to take advantage of it.' She rested one elbow on the chair arm and supported her chin, smiling ruefully. 'A wine producing business really needs a man at its head, even allowing for the present trend towards feminism, and the men take notice of someone like Eduardo. He's so strong and capable, I only wish he was running Casa Cortez as well as Anchoterrias!'

On the face of it it was a pretty provocative statement to make about a man to his bride, but Lari had little doubt that Juana Cortez made it without a qualm. She more than likely saw Lari as merely a minor irritation rather than a definite threat to her relationship with Eduardo, but if rousing her to irrational anger was the aim, then Lari determined it should fail.

'Even Eduardo would have difficulty being in two places at once,' she observed, and the dark eyes drooped their heavy lids as they looked at her.

'Not at all,' Juana denied with confidence, 'he'd be perfectly capable of it.' Her smile showed strong white teeth and her eyes were mocking. 'You obviously don't know your husband very well yet, *señora*, or you'd realise his capabilities. But then——'

The accompanying shrug conveyed even more than the words and Lari held on to her self-control determinedly. It was deliberate provocation and went beyond anything a sophisticated woman like Juana Cortez would have done when there were witnesses to her behaviour. Which was obviously why she had waited for Marta's departure before she indulged herself. Lari's only consolation was that she was so obviously driven by jealousy.

'In the meantime,' Juana went on smoothly, 'I know you won't mind my borrowing Eduardo himself from time to time, knowing how important it is that nothing goes wrong. You *won't* mind, will you?' she insisted, and took malicious note of Lari's swift flush of colour.

'That's something you'll have to talk to Eduardo

about,' she told her in as steady a voice as she could manage. 'I'm sure he'll do his best to find you a good *capataz, señora,* knowing how important it is. And he knows exactly what you want, of course.' Malice did not come easily to her, and she thought it was unexpected, although a woman like Juana Cortez was not to be outfaced for very long.

She sat for a moment longer, her eyes hidden, then slowly uncrossed her long slim legs and got up from her chair. She was graceful as a cat, Lari thought, and showed her claws with as much malice as any feline; and Lari hated her with a vehemence she would never have believed herself capable of.

'I'm sorry you've had such a—a disappointing journey, *señora,*' Lari told her, herself getting up. 'I'll tell him you called, and remind him about finding another *capataz.*'

Her smile barely curved the generous width of her mouth, and it glittered rather than warmed her dark eyes, as Juana Cortez smoothed her hands down the skirt of her elegant velvet suit. 'Oh, please don't trouble yourself about telling him,' she said. 'I'll call at the *bodegas* on my way and tell him myself. That's where he usually is at this time of day, isn't it?'

Lari grasped hastily at her rapidly slipping self-control, and somehow managed to force a smile, but her stomach felt churningly turbulent and to steady her hands she brushed them through her hair. 'You know the way?' she asked, as if nothing was further from her mind than a possible rendezvous between her husband and this woman, and Juana Cortez eyed her for a moment mockingly.

'I'll find it,' she assured her.

It was almost as if Marta made her appearance on cue, sharp-eyed, and carrying a tray bearing coffee for two and a plate of little fancy pastries. She placed the tray on a table beside the chair Lari had been sitting in and straightened up, her black gaze darting swiftly between Lari's flushed face and the inimical smile of the visitor. Whether or not coffee had been asked for, she had brought it.

'Señora?' she murmured, and Lari hastily pulled herself back to practicalities.

'Señora Cortez is just leaving, Marta, but I'll be glad of some coffee, thank you.'

'Señora.'

While Marta stood hovering, waiting to see her out, Juana proffered a hand in a token gesture of politeness, but her long cool fingers barely touched Lari's. 'I expect I'll see you again some time, Lari,' she said, and used her familiar first name with an air that challenged Lari to object to her using it. 'I may call you Lari, mayn't I?' she asked. 'I am family in a way, and I've known most of the Sagreras for more years than I care to remember.'

Lari accepted the unwelcome familiarity with a nod, but made no endeavour to return the compliment. Instead she murmured the platitude that years of Spanish protocol brought automatically to her tongue. 'Goodbye, *señora*; so good of you to call.'

A faint smile doubted its sincerity, and apparently her caller felt no such need to be polite. She said nothing, but turned and walked from the room with such staggering arrogance that Lari squeezed her hands into tight fists. She suspected Marta shared her emotion, for her back was straight and stiff as she led the way, and the moment the door closed behind them Lari bent and picked up a book from the table. Then quite deliberately she hurled it across the room with all the force she could muster, so that it crashed against the door and scattered its pages over the carpet.

'Bitch!' she declared fiercely, and was quite surprised to realise how much better she felt.

No mention was made of Juana Cortez's visit, and Lari wondered if Eduardo even knew the woman had called at the house, or whether Juana had eventually decided not to go to the *bodegas* in search of him after all. The latter was unlikely but not impossible, she thought.

Lari was never quite sure what prompted her to suggest she drive there with Eduardo the following morning, and she made allowances for his brief look of surprise when she suggested it. Almost as unexpected was the thrill of pleasure it gave her to ride beside him in the Land Rover, and she realised that whatever Juana Cortez said or did, nothing could alter the fact that he was *her* husband. And as they bounced and bumped along the dusty track to the *bodegas* she allowed herself a little smile of satisfaction.

Glancing from the corner of his eye Eduardo noticed the smile and turned his head, one brow arched enquiringly and his own mouth softened by a suggestion of smile. 'Something pleasing you?' he asked in the tone of voice that could, and did, do strange things to her senses, and Lari lowered her eyes before she answered.

'Nothing special,' she told him. 'I just felt like smiling, that's all; it's a happy kind of day.'

'I should hope so,' he smiled, and his voice drew caressing fingers down her back. 'You're very beautiful when you smile, Lari, you must do it more often, even though it makes you look alarmingly young!'

She obliged with a small, musing kind of smile as she glanced at him from the corners of her eyes, and felt more content than she had for some time. Acre on acre of vines ran in neat terraces both up and down hill and were heavy with the coming harvest, basking in the heat as she did herself. It was not only the heat that gave her cheeks their warm flush, though, but the nearness of the lean body that every bump in the track brought into closer contact, and the wild fancies she indulged in were much more erotic than ever before.

They approached the sprawling *bodegas* in the inevitable dust cloud that whirled into the small parking space behind them and settled on the body of the vehicle when they stopped. Reaching down to take her hand as she got out, Eduardo leaned suddenly and kissed her just beside her mouth, then laughed softly, as if her obvious surprise pleased him. A hand laid lightly on her forehead, he smiled.

'You feel very warm,' he murmured, clasping her fingers with his other hand. 'I wonder why! Never mind, you'll soon cool off when we get inside.'

In fact Lari shivered slightly as they walked into the vastness of the buildings that housed the maturing wine, and wondered at herself forgetting how chill the *bodegas* could be. Perhaps it was because she hadn't been for a while that she noticed it. Sometimes, when her stepfather had been taking a more active interest in the actual wine-making, she had come with him, but she had always been somewhat overawed by the vastness of them. Even now she found the sight of row on row of fat wooden barrels ranged in silent ranks below vaulted ceilings rather awe-inspiring.

Coming there with Eduardo wasn't quite the same because she felt somehow more involved, although she didn't see how that could be. She had no more of a proprietorial interest now than she had in her stepfather's time; but perhaps she was less overawed than she had once been. The head man had been with Sagrera and Sons for as long as Lari could remember, but he was obviously quite happy with his new employer, and that too was a source of satisfaction to her. A man who had been born into the wine business and knew it as thoroughly as Eduardo did commanded respect even among the old hands.

'How long is it since you were down here last, Lari?'

She walked beside him along the wide aisles that were only dimly lit from above, and she looked up at him curiously. *Had* Juana Cortez come to find him after all? she wondered. Try as she would, her discomfiting visitor of yesterday was hard to forget, and remembering coloured her reply.

'Quite a long time,' she admitted. 'But there was really no need with Luis Lopez in charge; he's very efficient, and it isn't really a woman's job, running a winery, is it?'

'I would say that rather depends on the woman,' he observed, and she thought he knew who she had in mind. 'But not you, Lari, you're not the businesslike type.'

'Did you mind me coming today?'

His curiously enigmatic smile could have meant anything, and she viewed it uneasily. 'Now why should you think that?' he countered.

Answering question with question was an annoying habit he had sometimes, and Lari frowned over it. 'No special reason,' she denied, 'I just wondered if you were one of those men who don't like women paying unexpected calls, unless it's in the way of business, of course.' His momentary silence suggested he knew what she referred to, and it made it that much more difficult to go on. 'That reminds me, did Señora Cortez call on you yesterday? She came to the house looking for you and when she was told you weren't there she said she'd come down here to look for you. It seemed pretty important from the way she spoke. You'd promised to find her another *capataz*, or something, she said.'

'I have said I'll do what I can to find her someone,' he agreed, and the lightness was gone from his voice she noticed, regretting it now that it was too late to change anything. He grasped her arm more tightly and there was a suggestion of cruelty in the grip that made her pulse more rapid and urgent suddenly. 'Is *that* why you came with me this morning, Lari? To check whether Juana had been to see me? If so, why did you not simply ask me at home?'

Colour made her cheeks burn furiously as Lari despairingly saw her earlier contentment rapidly dissolved because of one rash question. Drawing her arm free of that bruising grip, she blamed herself bitterly for having even mentioned Juana Cortez, but she couldn't help wondering just how often the other woman came to see him there without Lari ever knowing a thing about it. She had been so mockingly sure of herself when asked if she knew her way to the *bodegas*.

'I didn't think I needed a reason other than the fact that I felt like coming,' she told him, but she didn't sound nearly as convincing as she hoped. 'I suppose it was a bit thoughtless of me in the circumstances. Señora Cortez obviously knew her way down here and if she's—if you're expecting her——'

'I'm not,' Eduardo denied shortly, but anger put an edge of harshness on his voice and he was obviously in no mind to even consider she might be regretting the impression she had given. 'But with Juana it's difficult to forecast—like most women she's unpredictable!'

To Lari his qualifying the denial was the last straw, and she had never felt more small and uncertain in her life before. Head bent, she continued to walk alongside him, not knowing quite what else to do for the moment. 'I—I think it might be a good idea if I left you to get on—with whatever you have to do,' she told him. 'I can walk back, I've done it before.'

'Why, Lari?'

The demand took her off guard for a moment and she glanced up at him, trying to understand. 'I just think it might be best,' she said eventually. 'I know you're busy, and—well, I don't usually come here. I just didn't think this morning when I asked you.'

'You didn't think—about what, Lari?'

He stopped and with a hand on her arm swung her round in front of him so that she could see the dark look in his eyes. That particular aisle was deserted for the moment, and it gave the illusion of them being alone in the great cathedral-like cellars. The only signs of there being anyone else around was the abstract whisper of footsteps somewhere, and the murmur of disembodied voices, and the chill gloom of the *bodega* seemed to enter her heart as she looked at him.

'You're so sure that I bring my lover here, aren't you?' Eduardo demanded in a voice only a little less chill than the dim vaulted cellars, and Lari shivered. 'You're quite convinced of it, aren't you, Lari?'

'You—you haven't denied it,' she accused huskily, and while she prayed that he would, he still glowered at her darkly.

'Why should I trouble myself to deny something you seem to know all about?' he asked harshly, and Lari caught her breath, staring at him in stunned silence for a moment.

She felt numbly ice-cold in both mind and body, and the hardest of all was to find the effort to move. When she did, she snatched her arm free and turned from him swiftly, stumbling as she did so, and hurrying along a side aisle that led to the exit. Instinct alone guided her and she told herself she was a fool to react as she did to something she had been fully aware of before ever she came down there with him.

In the open air once more, she closed her eyes against the blinding glare of the sun, and brushed an impatient hand across them when she realised there were tears in them. She had said she didn't mind walking back, but seeing the Land Rover parked in a patch of shade just a few yards away, she made for it automatically, and she had one hand on the door ready to climb in when another vehicle pulled up immediately beside it.

She looked across at the sports car poised in a whirl of dust, and through the open window at a pair of huge dark eyes that watched her and speculated. 'Lari?'

Obviously the sight of her there was unexpected, and served to convince Lari that her suspicion had been right. There was an uncharacteristic air of restraint about Juana Cortez as she swung her long elegant legs out of the car, and quite automatically Lari noticed the shoes she was wearing.

They were unsuitably high-heeled for the uneven ground, and obviously very expensive, flattering to slender legs and ankles and made of crocodile skin. It should mean something, Lari thought, but at the moment her mind was too occupied with other matters. Like the fact that Juana Cortez had yet again come to see Eduardo, ostensibly to seek his advice, no doubt, and she felt a cold chilling bitterness that was hard to contain. She did not even make any kind of greeting as, undeterred by her obvious lack of welcome, the other woman eyed her curiously.

'You're an unexpected face to find down here,' Juana Cortez told her, and smoothed down her dress with a slightly nervous gesture that, in a more observant mood, would have surprised Lari. 'Is Eduardo about, Lari?'

Keeping control only with difficulty, Lari inclined her head towards the entrance to the *bodega*. She said nothing and was aware that the omission was noted, but she was shaking like a leaf as she climbed into the Land Rover. He had denied expecting Juana, but conceded that she might put in an appearance, and as she started the engine Lari hated her husband and his lover with all the passion and fury she was capable of. But she was crying too, and that was less easy to explain.

Lunch was the main meal of the day, and Lari had

been quite looking forward to it while she and Eduardo had their truce; now she dreaded sitting down at the same table with him. He came in at his usual time and cast her a swift, meaningful glance when he came to push in her chair, bringing the customary flutter of reaction when his hands brushed her arms, lightly and evocatively.

They ate baked fish and its accompanying sauce in complete silence, and only when Marta served them with generously seasoned stewed chicken did either of them speak. 'I vowed I wouldn't say a word until you did,' Eduardo informed her the moment Marta closed the *salón* door behind her, 'but it's such a childish thing to do and I at least should be too mature to indulge in it.'

Not quite sure what was expected of her, Lari got on with her meal, but glanced up briefly at him. He caught her eye and the sudden thud of emotion she felt in her heart made her immediately tearful again, although she subdued it hastily. 'I—I hope I am too,' she said.

It was difficult not to jump when he curved long gentle fingers over hers and squeezed them lightly. 'Try again?' he suggested, and Lari swallowed hard.

'Would it work?' she countered, in a small voice, for it was very hard to forget Juana Cortez strutting so boldly across the *bodega* car park in search of him.

Another brief glance showed a tightness about his mouth, and made her doubt it would ever work, but she wanted desperately to try. 'I rather think that depends on you,' Eduardo told her, and she had it in mind to remind him that it was his friend who was the cause of their disagreeing, not hers. Only she really did want to make it up with him, and she might be able to put Juana Cortez to the back of her mind if she tried very hard. 'Lari?'

The gentle prompt was all she needed, and Lari was

already nodding her head when she heard voices in the hall. Eduardo heard them too, and he was frowning, recognising the less familiar one, just as she did herself. A man's voice, cool and crisp and speaking English with a hint of impatience because he was not being understood, and Marta was trying to tell him they were still at lunch.

'Eric Truman!' she breathed, but scarcely believed it even though she recognised his voice, and she saw Eduardo's frown deepen to a scowl.

'I wish to see Señora Sagrera, *please* go and find her and tell her I'm here!'

The voice persisted, clear and unmistakable, and Lari rued his insistence but felt helpless to do anything about it. His frown was directed at the door into the hall, but Eduardo's glance darted swiftly and briefly to Lari, the look in his eyes dark and stormy as he got to his feet. 'Holy Mother!' he declared in a tight harsh voice. 'You have the temerity to accuse me of having a lover, and your—Englishman comes calling at our home demanding to see you!'

'I didn't know he was coming!' Her defensiveness was instinctive, not planned, and in her heart she wished Eric Truman anywhere but out there in the hall asking to see her.

'Obviously not, or you wouldn't look so startled!' Eduardo retorted. 'He must be very lacking in the discretion the English so pride themselves on! Where are you going?' he demanded when she half rose from her chair.

'To—to ask him to go away.'

He pressed a hand on her shoulder until she sat down again, and stood towering over her looking the very personification of the outraged husband, and there was a curious curling sensation in her stomach when she met fierce black eyes. He flung down his table napkin and his chair scraped back on the wood-brick floor, and she looked up at him anxiously.

'Eduardo, what are you going to do?'

'Tell him to stay away from my wife!' he informed her harshly. 'It seems you haven't been discouraging enough!' His dark eyes blazed fiercely at the very idea of someone else daring to even approach what he considered his property, and he was lean and taut as a bowstring. 'I won't have my wife's reputation put in jeopardy because some romantic idiot fancies himself in love!'

'How do you know it's only fancy?'

He was at the door when she hurled her defiance at him, and he stopped with one hand actually on the handle. When he turned, he turned slowly, and something in his expression set her heart thudding wildly, making her place her hands together with the fingertips resting on her chin, not knowing what to make of that cold yet passionate look he turned on her.

As so often happens when two people speaking different languages try to communicate, the voices in the hall grew louder, and Eric Truman's words reached them clear and distinct. 'Oh, for God's sake, how can I make you understand? I have something to give to the *señora* personally! I promised I'd sign one and let her have it personally.'

It was the clue Lari needed, for she thought she understood at last why Eric Truman had risked her husband's wrath to come and ask for her, and she called out to him as she got to her feet. 'Eduardo!' Black eyes questioned her appeal and were, she believed, briefly moved by it, but she remained where she was for the moment. 'I think he's probably brought me a copy of his latest book,' she explained. 'He promised me a signed copy.'

'Then I'll accept it on your behalf,' he told her.

He didn't quite close the door behind him so that Lari heard the ensuing exchange quite clearly. 'Oh, thank goodness for someone who speaks English!' Eric Truman said in obvious relief when Eduardo appeared. 'Good afternoon, Señor Sagrera, I've been trying to make your lady here understand that I'd like to see Señora Sagrera for a minute.'

'May I ask why, *señor*?'

There was no sign of that fierce passion now, Lari noted, only an almost chill politeness that she could imagine would deter all but the most persistent; and Eric Truman, she feared, might prove to be just that. 'I promised your wife a copy of my book,' he explained. 'I have it here.'

'You're very generous, *señor*,' Eduardo's deep chill voice told him. 'First a bouquet of carnations and now a book—most generous, but in Spanish eyes rather indiscreet, Señor Truman. Fortunately I am an understanding husband.'

From the ensuing silence it was clear that Eric Truman was unsure of his opponent. 'Will you—may I leave it with you?'

'Of course,' Eduardo agreed coldly pedantic. 'But we are at present eating lunch, *señor*——'

'Oh yes, I see, I didn't realise.' Eduardo must have been fully aware of the embarrassment he caused by stressing the fact that he had interrupted their meal, and Lari recalled the suggestion of cruelty she had sometimes noticed in the firm line of his mouth. 'In that case I'd better leave the book.'

It must surely have been deliberate too that the door had been left just sufficiently wide open that she could be seen through the opening, sitting at the table and looking far from happy with the situation. Eric Truman caught sight of her and his eyes narrowed slightly not bothering to hide the fact that he had seen her. He still had the book in his hand and because she feared he might be impulsive enough to risk annoying Eduardo to bring it to her, she got quickly to her feet and came out into the hall to join them.

'Thank you, Señor Truman.' She spoke as she came up behind Eduardo, and ignored his swift frown of disapproval as she smilingly took the book from its donor. 'That's very kind of you, thank you.'

Quite obviously, for all his air of bravado, he found Eduardo rather overwhelming, for he shrugged uneasily and glanced at his wristwatch. 'I do apologise for interrupting your meal, but I've never got used to Spanish mealtimes.' He extended a hand to Lari. 'I hope you like the book, Señora Sagrera; perhaps when we meet again you'll give me your opinion of it.'

'I'll be delighted to,' Lari assured him before Eduardo could say whatever he had been going to, 'and thank you so much for bringing it, Señor Truman.'

The enclosing fingers squeezed hard for a moment, and his grey eyes managed to hold hers, glowing warmly in a way that Eduardo was hardly likely to miss. 'Couldn't you make it Eric?' he suggested, and Lari felt Eduardo stiffen at the suggestion of intimacy, not only in the suggestion but in his voice too. 'We *are* compatriots,' he stressed, then seemed to realise how tactless he was being and hastened to amend the invitation. 'I'd like it if you used my first name too, if you will, Señor Sagrera, we are neighbours after all.'

Eduardo took the hand he proffered and inclined his head slightly, but he yielded not an inch on the matter of becoming more familiar. 'It is kind of you to present my wife with a copy of your book, *señor*,' he told him. 'I am sure it will be appreciated—*adios*, Señor Truman.'

Just for a moment a frown drew Eric's light brows together, and it was clear that he realised he had been firmly rebuffed, however politely. Then he was smiling again, and looking directly at Lari once more, his feelings undisguised. 'I'm sure we'll meet again, *señora,* but until we do——' He reached for her hand and raised it to his lips, pressing them lightly, not once but several times to her fingertips. 'It's only *au revoir,* I hope.'

Lari merely smiled; let him think she echoed his hope if it pleased him. Ignoring Eduardo's obvious dislike of it, she walked to the door with her visitor and stood watching while he started his car, then waved a hand as he drove away. In her present mood it wasn't Eric Truman who was important to her, but the effect he had on Eduardo, and even then she recognised how unwise it would be to allow things to go too far.

Eduardo's stormy dark eyes followed her while she walked back to him, and the moment she got within reach he laid a hand on her arm; not roughly, as she half expected, but lightly so that she shivered slightly at its touch and looked up at him. 'He means to take you from me,' he said, and the flat conviction in his voice startled her.

'Oh no, Eduardo!'

'You think I don't know men?' he demanded. 'And the most insulting part of it is, he thinks I don't realise it!' His eyes gleamed darkly, stirring those curious responses in her again. 'How else could he find the nerve to come here so boldly and look at you as he does? Kissing your hand as a lover would and begging that you use his first name! Sending you flowers, giving you books!'

Lari was trembling like a leaf, every nerve in her body reacting to the passion that thickened his voice and gave his features a look of harshness, because she wanted to believe he spoke as he did out of jealousy. Nevertheless she kept recent events in mind and took nothing for granted.

'He probably thinks it's the polite thing to do in Spain, to kiss a woman's hand,' she suggested, and her eyes darted upward as she said it. They might almost have carried an image of Juana Cortez in their depths, so clearly did they convey her meaning. 'And he did only kiss my hand, Eduardo, not my mouth.'

'If he dares——' Eduardo began, but Lari cut him short, a little surprised at her own boldness and recognising none of the myriad emotions that churned inside her.

'Oh, I don't doubt he'll dare when he's known me a little longer!' she told him. 'He probably thinks he has the God-given right to kiss any woman who takes his fancy—like you in a way, I suppose, which is most likely why you dislike him so much! There's always a little added excitement, I imagine, about kissing someone else's wife that you don't find in your own!'

The words were scarcely out of her mouth before she was gasping for breath at being pulled forcibly against the taut angry leanness of him, murmuring protest at the steely hardness of fingers around her upper arms. Looking up was instinctive, and it gave him her mouth like an offering, the soft lips parted in the beginning of a protest that was never voiced. Instead he took them with cruel force, his mouth bruisingly hard, searching and demanding, stunning in its fierceness and unbelievably exciting.

Yet she had barely time to respond to the excitement of being more close to him than ever before, before he let her go. Free of his mouth and the steely grip of his hands, she made no attempt to move away; unwilling to lose the excitement of his proximity that seemed so much more desirable than ever before.

'Whatever the reason for our marrying,' he declared in a deep and not quite steady voice, 'I alone have the privileges of a husband, and if ever I find that Englishman taking what is mine, I'll——'

He left the actual threat unsaid, but the burning fierceness in his eyes made her tremble, even though his expressed reason for making it was more possessive than romantic. Shaking her head, Lari despaired of her own growing love for him ever being given a chance to flourish. What chance was there with Juana Cortez laying claim to his affections and Eduardo himself regarding her as another possession, like Anchoterrias? 'I think you're wrong about his motives,' she told him, but Eduardo was adamant.

'I think not,' he insisted. 'But whether or not he gets the message is entirely up to you in the long run, Lari, and you'd better make it quite clear to him!'

If only he realised how much it was up to him, Lari thought as they moved back into the *salón* to continue their lunch, and she glanced up briefly as he ushered her before him into the room. 'I'll do my best,' she promised, though without much conviction, she feared.

Harlequin Romances

Thrill to romantic, aristocratic Istanbul, and the tender love story of a girl who built a barrier around her emotions in ANNE HAMPSON'S "Beyond the Sweet Waters"... a Caribbean island is the serene setting for love and conflict in ANNE MATHER'S "The Arrogant Duke"... exciting, sun-drenched California is the locale for romance and deception in VIOLET WINSPEAR'S "Cap Flamingo"... and an island near the coast of East Africa spells drama and romance for the heroine in NERINA HILLIARD'S "Teachers Must Learn."

Harlequin Romances... 6 exciting novels published each month! Each month you will get to know interesting, appealing, true-to-life people... You'll be swept to distant lands you've dreamed of visiting... Intrigue, adventure, romance, and the destiny of many lives will thrill you through each Harlequin Romance novel.

Get all the latest books before they're sold out!

As a Harlequin subscriber you actually receive your personal copies of the latest Romances immediately after they come off the press, so you're sure of getting all 6 each month.

Cancel your subscription whenever you wish!

You don't have to buy any minimum number of books. Whenever you decide to stop your subscription just let us know and we'll cancel all further shipments.

CHAPTER FIVE

LARI had seen nothing more of Eric Truman since that rather disturbing lunchtime incident, and she hoped he would never be so indiscreet again. She had read his book and found it even more frankly earthy than Marta's warning had led her to expect, although she had to concede that it was well written and was almost certainly destined to become a best-seller.

Rather to her surprise Eduardo had asked to borrow it and, knowing he had finished reading it the night before, she sought his opinion. 'Did you like the book?' she ventured, and he regarded her in silence for a moment.

'Did you?' he countered, indulging yet again in that annoying habit of answering question with question.

Not quite knowing how frank to be, Lari hesitated. 'I—it isn't my usual sort of reading,' she told him eventually, and he laughed shortly before she could go on.

'I should hope not! God knows I'm no prude, but that isn't the sort of thing I'd present to a young woman, and particularly when she happens to be someone else's wife!'

'Well, he'd probably think that was rather an old-fashioned view,' she suggested.

'And do *you* think so?' Eduardo demanded, eyeing her narrowly. 'Somehow I don't quite see a sex novel as in the same class as flowers or a box of chocolates a love token, so maybe I am old-fashioned as you suggest. I only hope he doesn't present you with a copy of his next one too!'

She watched his face through her lashes for a second, speculating. 'Would you try to stop me reading it?' she asked, remembering Marta's suggestion that he wouldn't like her having such reading matter in the house.

Eduardo said nothing for a moment, and she wondered if he really would try to take a hand in choosing what she read. 'Difficult as it is for me to realise it,' Eduardo said eventually, 'you are a grown woman, Lari, and as you've already said it isn't your usual taste, I don't think I need say anything, do you?'

It wasn't a very satisfactory answer, but Lari was disinclined to follow it up, so she said nothing. They ate in silence for several minutes, while Lari tried to decide whether or not she would ever defy him on the matter of Eric Truman's books if it came to the point. She thought not, she decided, and picked a safer subject than Eric Truman when she spoke again.

'Did you mean it when you said you were going to have the house completely redecorated?' she asked, and Eduardo nodded. 'But does it really need it, Eduardo?'

'I think so or I wouldn't have suggested it,' he told her, 'and you must admit that it needs it, Lari. Oh, it may not be quite so evident to you, being here all the time, but to someone coming in from outside as I have, it looks very shabby.'

Looking at the old house, half buried in its surrounding trees, Lari had to admit that it might be in need of some renovation, and she nodded agreement. 'I suppose it does,' she allowed.

The soft shadows cast by the trees on the *patio* added depth to the contours of his face, and a light shirt showed broad shoulders and the darkness of bronzed flesh through its texture. He was a strong and sensual man for all he treated her so coolly, a man that most women would find attractive, and Lari wanted nothing more than to love him as she knew she could if only he gave her an ounce of encouragement.

She looked at the bare brown arms and powerful

hands and recalled the thrill of being held tightly in them, then she remembered Juana Cortez and Eduardo's refusal to deny he was having an affair with her. Dreams like that belonged in the age she had left behind with her teens; her best plan now was to keep both feet firmly on the ground.

'While the decorating is being done,' Eduardo said, breaking into her daydream, 'we'll move to Santa Inés, as Padre has suggested, and give the workmen a free hand. I'll see Paco Montez this morning and see how soon he can start.'

Lari was staring at him in dismay, making little or no effort to hide her feelings regarding a move to Santa Inés. 'Is that necessary?' she asked. 'I mean, we could manage——'

'No doubt we could,' Eduardo conceded, 'but I don't relish being hounded from room to room, and it won't take nearly as long if the house is empty. Marta can stay and keep an eye on things, and I'll be driving over here every day, of course.' He caught sight of her expression suddenly and frowned. 'For heaven's sake, Lari, don't look like that! We shall be spending a few weeks with my family, that's all!'

As if spending several weeks with his formidable family wasn't bad enough, Lari thought despairingly, but more than likely Juana Cortez would still be there too. It was a prospect that frankly appalled her, and yet she did not anticipate that her feelings would be taken into account even if she voiced them; which she did nevertheless.

'I suppose Señora Cortez will still be there?' she said, and saw the quick tightening of his mouth.

'I imagine so,' he agreed, and the bright darkness of his eyes when he looked across at her was a direct challenge. 'But I don't imagine Eric Truman will be arriving at Santa Inés with bouquets of carnations and lurid books, do you?' His smile was taut and humourless and slightly crooked. 'Could be you misjudged my motive, Lari?' he suggested drily.

'I don't think so!' She could almost happily spend a lifetime with her in-laws if she thought his motive had been jealousy of Eric Truman, but she was too sure that it was pride and possessiveness not love that moved him. 'And if you're really concerned about your good name, Eduardo, you should think about your—affair with Juana Cortez instead of Eric Truman. Not that I have any interest in what you get up to with your lady-friend, but if word got around——'

'I think you've said enough!'

He got to his feet and stood for a moment looking down at her, a faint frown drawing at his brows. Tall and almost menacing, he towered over her and every nerve in her body responded to him in a way she had no control over. Her heart clamoured wildly at the raw masculine vigour of him until she felt it must surely be evident in the fluttering paleness of her breast where her dress gaped.

'How could I have been so sure that I knew you?' he asked, in a voice that suggested he addressed the question to himself rather than to her.

'Eduardo——'

He turned swiftly and left her, striding off across the *patio* while Lari watched him go and gnawed anxiously on her lower lip. If only she could come to terms with the fact that her marriage was one of convenience only and had nothing whatever to do with love, it would be so much easier for them both. Instead she cared too much, and his affair with Juana Cortez made her both angry and unhappy.

When Marta heard the news that she was to be left in charge while the house was redecorated, and that Lari and Eduardo were to move temporarily to Santa Inés, she did her best to make light of Lari's obvious reluctance. She offered sympathy and understanding, but at the same time tried to encourage her to accept the inevitable.

'It won't be for very long, little one,' she told her, using an endearment that had followed on from childhood. 'And Señor Eduardo is quite right about it being by far the most convenient arrangement; it will mean that the men have the free run of the house and will be done that much sooner.'

'But they hate me, Marta! You know the Sagreras have never liked my mother or me! If it wasn't for that wretched will of Papá's they'd never have had anything more to do with me, you know that, Marta! And so does Eduardo, only——'

'Señora, señora!' Marta stopped her from becoming too indiscreet but Lari needed someone to open her heart to and there was no one but Marta. 'I'm quite sure no one hates you,' Marta insisted, but even she could not argue with the truth of her next statement, and Lari knew it.

'I won't believe that Juana Cortez doesn't hate me,' she said, and watched the way Marta's heavy lids suddenly concealed the look in her eyes. 'And you know why, Marta, don't you?' She sighed and clasped her hands together, exasperated by her own helplessness, 'If she wasn't going to be there too, I might have survived a week or two with the Sagreras.' Marta was silent, but even her silence seemed pregnant with meaning so that Lari looked at her curiously. 'Marta, just who *is* Señora Cortez? Oh, I know she's the widow of some obscure cousin of my mother-in-law's, but what else is she?'

'Señor Cortez was not—obscure, *señora,* he was a very wealthy man and a well-known one in wine circles.'

She was being evasive, Lari recognised, and that in itself was enough to make her more curious and more determined to discover just who or what Juana Cortez was. 'Tell me, Marta.'

The old woman seemed to be weighing up the advisability of imparting what she knew, and Lari's stomach fluttered anxiously when she realised it. 'I'm not sure Señor Eduardo would want me to tell you, *señora*.'

'I don't care what Eduardo wants,' Lari told her sharply. 'I have a feeling that Juana Cortez and I are going to become even more involved once we're under the same roof, and I want to know exactly who it is I'm up against!'

'There's little enough to tell,' Marta demurred, accepting the inevitable. 'She was Señorita Mateos before she married, and when she realised that he would not be such a good catch because of Señor José remarrying, she ended the association and married elsewhere; Señor Cortez being a better prospect. A third share in a business isn't like the whole thing, and Señorita Mateos was not one to take second best. Of course whether or not there was ever a firm engagement, I don't know, there's some doubt about that, I think.'

Lari's head was spinning, and she could not quite bring herself to believe what was whirling around in her brain. 'You—you're telling me that she—jilted somebody because he wasn't as rich as she hoped, and married Señor Cortez instead?'

'That's right, *señora*.' The gyspy black eyes watched her, their expression impossible to decipher. 'There are three brothers, you see, and it isn't such a big estate as Anchoterrias for all it's very profitable; divided into three it wouldn't have been nearly enough for that young lady!'

'But——' Lari licked her dry lips anxiously, trying already to come to terms with what she strongly suspected she was going to hear. 'Who—who was it she was engaged to, Marta.'

'Why,' Marta said as if she did not believe her so slow, 'to Señor Eduardo, of course!'

Lari found her mother-in-law even more difficult to get along with than she had anticipated, mostly she supposed because they had so little common ground. Señora Sagrera senior was suspicious of her being English too, however well Lari spoke her language, and she never unbent to her as she sometimes did to her Spanish daughter-in-law.

Of course the wife of Eduardo's youngest brother was a quiet and unassuming young woman, obedient and amenable to the rather autocratic old lady's will. Also she had already given her husband two sons and was expecting a third child, while in contrast Lari and Eduardo did not even share the same bedroom—a state of affairs that so shocked the old lady that she had raised her hands in horror and called on the saints to witness her despair.

Juana Cortez was, on the other hand, a welcome guest and treated as such, a fact that Juana herself never failed to bring to Lari's notice without making it too obvious to anyone else. It still made Lari feel almost physically sick when she thought of Eduardo once having been engaged to her, and living again under the same roof. How could he be so insensitive, even if theirs was a marriage in name only?

It was with the idea of escaping the stifling atmosphere of Santa Inés for a few hours that Lari asked Eduardo if she could drive over to Anchoterrias one morning. She didn't have her own car there, but she could quite easily drive over with him and wait for him to bring her back in the evening; no one was likely to miss her, and Marta would be quite glad of her company, she thought.

He was willing enough to take her, though he looked a little surprised when she asked him initially. 'What will you do with yourself all day?' he asked, and she smiled.

'Much as I always did at home,' she told him.

They were driving along the valley road and all along it she caught glimpses of the old house among its trees, brief promises that already made her feel better and more lighthearted. It would be such a relief to be free of her mother-in-law for a few hours, and most of all free of the smoothly malicious presence of Juana Cortez, although she went off somewhere most days for a few hours, and Lari gathered from her mother-in-law that she visited various relatives and friends, as well as the occasional shopping trip to Seville with Elena Sagrera.

'Will you find it as easy to keep yourself amused with the house upside down?' Eduardo asked, and she nodded.

'Quite easily,' she assured him. 'There'll be plenty to talk about too.'

'You mean to Marta?'

Lari glanced at him from the corner of her eye, puzzled by his mood. 'Who else?' she asked, and noticed how quickly he turned his head away, regretting it more than she cared to admit because it raised old ghosts she had hoped were forgotten. And his silence seemed to suggest he had a suspicion that she had a motive for coming other than the obvious one. 'I'm not seeing Eric Truman, if that's what you're thinking, Eduardo,' she promised, and this time his eyes met hers squarely. 'You just can't forget that he—fancies himself in love with me, can you?'

'You yourself hinted that it might not *be* fancy,' he reminded her, and Lari shook her head over something she had regretted more than once since she was [illegible]h enough to have said it.

Glancing at his dark enigmatic face, she sighed inwardly. 'That was mostly your fault,' she told him.

'Oh? How so?'

'Because you suggested it *was* only fancy,' she told him, encouraged by a ghost of a smile. 'It seemed to imply that you couldn't imagine him actually being in love with me, and it wasn't really very complimentary, you know.'

'It wasn't meant to be derogatory either; if it seemed so, I'm sorry.'

His apology and the half-smile on his mouth made it easier to make light of it, and the tilt of her brows was more pert than challenging. 'Feminine pride,' she assured him, 'is a very delicate thing.'

'So I'm discovering!'

'And I like to feel I'm trusted,' she went on. 'There is no way that Eric Truman can know I'll be here today, will you accept that?'

'Willingly!' His smile brought a responding warmth to her heart and she mellowed in it like a flower in the sun. 'And I shall trust you to check on what progress the workmen are making,' Eduardo went on, 'instead of doing it myself; does that satisfy your feminine pride?'

Lari laughed without any real reason for doing so. 'Oh, I'll make sure they're getting on with it!' she assured him. 'You can count on it!'

Anchoterrias sprawled its green acres over the hillside, and as they approached it Lari wished there was some way she could persuade Eduardo to let her stay, instead of going back to Santa Inés. But she hesitated to suggest it because she cherished their present harmony too much to risk spoiling it.

'If I come for you about two o'clock, would you like to drive into Seville for lunch?' Eduardo asked, and Lari turned quickly, stunned by the unexpectedness of it for a moment. Then, shiny-eyed, she hastened to accept.

'Oh yes, I'd love to, Eduardo!'

It didn't matter that she sounded almost childlike in her eagerness to accept, for she only now realised that it was the very first time he had taken her out for a meal, and as he turned on to the dusty track through the vineyard, Lari knew she had never been happier in her life; even if she did have to go back to Santa Inés for a while.

'Don't get out, I can manage!' She stopped him coming round to open the car door for her, and on impulse, leaned across with a hand on his arm to plant a kiss on his cheek. ''Bye,' she said happily, 'see you about two!'

She slid across the seat and would have swung her legs out of the car, but there were strong fingers twined in her hair suddenly and a gentle pull brought her tipping backwards until she lay against him with her face turned upward and her lips parted. He laid an arm across her, just under the curve of her breasts and long fingers spanned upward with caressing firmness, holding her while he bent his head and stopped her uneven breath with his mouth.

The hard warm virility of him stirred her senses wildly while his fingers in her hair held her head still. Her eyes closed, she felt the pounding of her heart like a drum beat, and the need to press closer still made her half turn towards him in the steely arm that encircled her. It could have been only a second or two, and yet it seemed an interminable time before she breathed again.

When she opened her eyes Eduardo was looking down at her and from that angle it was hard to say what his expression was exactly. But there was a burning darkness in his eyes that made them gleam like polished jet, and while she was still trying to recover her breath the encircling arm drew her upright again.

Heart beating wildly and her cheeks flushed, Lari half turned towards him, but he must have misjudged her silence because he made a sound that was something between a sigh and a laugh. 'That was something I couldn't resist!' he said, putting a helping hand at her back as she got out of the car. 'Be ready, Lari, I'll be back for you at two!'

It was difficult to think clearly and Lari stood with the car door still open and one hand resting on it, feeling flushed and trembling and slightly lightheaded. He seemed unaware of how a kiss like that could affect her, and if he had realised, she thought hazily, he would probably mock her for being so naïve.

'I have a lot to do,' he told her, and his eyes were dark and unfathomable between their thick lashes, his voice gentle and quiet, seeking to reassure her. And she knew when she heard it that he would never have mocked her for feeling as she did, because he had used that same gentle tone to her when she was a small girl. 'Close the door, little one,' he told her, 'and let me get on.'

'You won't forget about me?'

The plea was impulsive, but her eyes were anxious, and he smiled, a smile that did violent things to her pulse and showed strong even teeth for a moment. Leaning across, he closed the door himself, then remained resting on one hand while he looked at her, a slow and infinitely disturbing study, with his shadowed eyes lingering for a moment at the open neck of her dress before he sat back.

'I won't forget you, Lari,' he promised. 'But I really do have a lot to do this morning and I must go. I'll see you at two, O.K.?'

'O.K.!'

Lari watched him go, waving a hand as the big car was swallowed up in its accompanying dust devil. If only they hadn't to go back to Santa Inés there might be a chance for them; a chance that things would be as she had always dreamed they could be. But today was promising and who knew? Perhaps tomorrow would be even better.

Apparently Marta was more or less confined to the kitchen quarters while the decorators were in occupation, and she apologised for having no other place to take her when she arrived. From the sound of men's voices all over the house it seemed the whole place was taken over by painters and paperers.

Lari was much less concerned with the rightness of things than with how much longer the work was going to take, and she dismissed Marta's apologies, insisting that she was quite happy to have her coffee in the kitchen. But they had barely time to settle to conversation before the doorbell rang and Marta went grumblingly to answer it.

Whether or not she would have admitted Eric Truman or sent him away none the wiser about Lari being there was debatable, but as it happened Lari came out to see who the caller was; half hoping to find that Eduardo had found himself less busy than he anticipated.

Eric Truman's eyes gleamed the way they always did when he saw her, and it was very difficult to resist that warming smile. 'Lari!' He had obviously taken the matter of first names for granted, although his use of hers with Marta listening, gave her a moment' uneasiness.

'Good morning, Eric.' She ignored Marta's disapproving eye for the moment, in a quandary to know what to do about him. After her earlier conversation with Eduardo he was doubly unwelcome, and yet she did not feel she could simply snub him and send him away without some kind of explanation. 'I—I'm afraid we're in rather a mess, we have the workmen in.'

'I heard you had,' he said. 'I also heard you'd moved out while the work was being done, but then I noticed you go past in your husband's car this morning and thought I'd come over on the off-chance.'

'Eduardo comes here every day, I came over with him this morning for a change.' She was still trying to come to terms with the idea of entertaining him in the kitchen under Marta's disapproving eye, and just didn't see how she could. 'I'm sorry, but there simply——'

'Not to worry!' he told her, and caught the malevolent glare that Marta gave him before going back to the kitchen. 'Look, why don't we drive down into the village and have a drink? Your husband will be at the works—or whatever, won't he?'

Ruing the mischance that had made him notice her arrival, Lari shook her head. 'I can't Eric, I'm sorry. Eduardo definitely wouldn't like me going with you; quite reasonably in the circumstances.'

'He doesn't trust me?' His expression was a curious blend of naïvety and wiliness, and it made her uneasy. 'Well, I don't blame him; in his position I wouldn't trust me either, and with good cause!'

'Please don't!' She was at a loss and admitted it readily to herself; the situation was one new to her and she didn't quite know how to handle it. 'I—I think it might be better if you went,' she ventured, not wanting to sound too inhospitable but seeing herself with no alternative in the circumstances.

The grey eyes were speculative, she recognised, assessing her sincerity and perhaps seeing her more tempted than she was. 'I'm quite potty about you, you know that, don't you?' he asked with a half-smile, and Lari's cheeks flooded with colour as she shook her head. 'Just one little drink, Lari?'

More desperate to be rid of him than she would have

believed possible, Lari shook her head. 'No—thank you! Whether or not mine is a marriage of convenience, *señor*, I have no intention of being unfaithful to my husband!'

She realised only when she saw his expression how rashly frank she had been in her agitation, but it served to make him withdraw his hand from her arm as he stared at her in obvious disbelief. 'My God!' he breathed, and rubbed a hand over his head in growing abhorrence. 'Oh, my God, I can't believe this! You're —you *are* English?' He didn't wait for confirmation but went on in a voice that shook with heaven knew what emotions, 'And yet you married Sagrera for—for what?'

It was not his concern, no matter what motivated his anger, and Lari meant to tell him so; kindly and reasonably, because she believed he genuinely felt for her, but firmly, so that he would be in no doubt where he stood. 'My reason need not concern you, Señor Truman,' she told him, thinking it more politic to keep it formal. 'I'm married and I've no intention of deceiving my husband.'

'I just don't believe this!'

'I don't see why you should assume that the—the situation automatically entitles me to be unfaithful,' Lari reasoned, though her voice was far more unsteady than she liked. 'Now will you please——'

'You can't be happy, for God's sake!' he objected, and his eyes were bright and angry, though whether she or Eduardo was the object of it Lari couldn't be sure. 'You know he plays around with——'

'I must ask you to go, Señor Truman—*please*!'

He ran his hands through his hair, and Lari's fear at the moment was that Marta would come and discover the situation she had got herself into, and yet she half wished she would come. Eric Truman was shaking his head and it occurred to Lari that he just could not believe her serious. He was very good-looking and probably used to getting what he wanted; the fact that he could make no headway in her case must be hard to take, apart from any genuine concern he felt for her.

'If only you knew how I've wanted you, all those weeks and months when I kept away because of your stepfather,' he mourned. 'And as if it wasn't bad enough coming back to find you married, you tell me it's not really a marriage at all! God, what I couldn't do to that tight-mouthed Spanish tyrant for tying you to him and then flaunting his woman in front of you, even at your wedding reception!'

'*Señor*——'

'I won't budge until you assure me he doesn't—My God, if he as much as lays a finger on you, I'll kill him!'

His violence was alarming, but oddly petulant and quite unlike Eduardo's fiery temper. He probably would resort to hitting Eduardo if he was provoked far enough, but she would not have been surprised to find him rather more verbal than active. She was beginning to despair of her ability to handle the situation when she heard a car stop, and having the advantage of seeing the newcomer through the open door, Lari felt her heart sink. There could surely be nothing more disastrous, she thought bitterly, than to be caught like this by Juana Cortez.

'Señor Truman——' she began, but he cut her short, taking her hands and holding them too tightly for her to escape.

'Don't you realise how I feel?' he pleaded, but Lari was too much aware of Juana's expression as she came in through the partly open door.

The first impression was one of stunned disbelief, and then the more familiar malice gleamed from dark eyes as she came straight in without hesitation, her high heels clicking on the tiled hall floor and distracting Eric Truman's attention at last. Dark red lips parted in a mockery of a smile as she took stock of the situation, and curled derisively when Lari struggled to free her hands.

'Lari, I didn't know you were going to be here, I thought you'd be with Eduardo. Does he know you have company?'

Lari's tongue moistened her lips while she rubbed at the marks his fingers had left. 'Señor Truman is our nearest neighbour,' she said, speaking English for his sake. 'He was at our wedding reception, do you remember? Eric, this is Señora Cortez, a—a distant cousin of my husband's. Señora Cortez——'

She had slipped up, using his first name, Lari realised when she saw Juana take note of it. 'Not so distant that you can't use *my* first name too,' she interrupted in surprisingly good English. She smiled archly at him, and extended a hand which Eric Truman took in something of a daze. 'Of course I know all about *you*, Señor Truman!'

In her confusion Lari momentarily forgot about his claim to fame as an author and her first thought was that Eduardo had told Juana Cortez about Eric's pursuit of her. She squirmed inwardly at the very idea, until Eric's own reaction reminded her of the more likely meaning.

He recovered something of his smooth charm and half-smiled into those huge dark eyes, inclining his head slightly at the same time. 'I'm flattered that you know about me, *señora*; of course I remember you quite well.' He gave Lari a swift calculating look from the corner of his eye. 'I seem to remember that you were talking to the bridegroom for quite a long time.'

'While you walked away with the bride!' Juana countered swiftly, and laughed as if she found the idea amusing. 'You have no idea how much you shocked two very proper old aunts, *señor*!'

Eric's grey eyes gleamed and he apparently saw no call for discretion where his feelings were concerned. 'I imagine they would have been considerably more shocked if they'd realised how shattered I was when I came back from a couple of weeks in England and found Lari married,' he declared, and while Lari caught her breath, Juana Cortez looked definitely interested.

'Shattered?' She evidently did not quite understand for a moment, his use of the word in that context. 'Ah, do you mean that you were—distressed, Señor Truman? But surely not on such short acquaintance! Do the English become so quickly distressed when they learn that strangers have married?'

Eric began to realise where it was leading and the possible consequences for Lari, and he darted an anxious tongue over his lips as he glanced at her again. 'That's exaggerating it a bit, *señora,*' he told her, and laughed a little uneasily. 'Perhaps—an author's taste for the dramatic, say. Every situation is a possible plot.'

'And such a plot in your latest book!' Juana remarked, rolling her fine eyes meaningly. 'If you took such a tale from personal experience, *señor*, you are a very wicked man, *no*? Tell me, who was your inspiration for such a passionate story?' Her eyes had a deceptively ingenuous look for a moment, though it deceived nobody in fact, least of all the man it was directed at. 'Was it Lari, perhaps? Have you possibly known her for longer than any of us realise?'

'Oh no, indeed, *señora*!'

'Oh? And yet you were—shattered?—when you returned to Spain and found that she was married?'

Eric could not know how much was at stake, but Lari realised exactly, and she was shaking like a leaf. What he had said already to Juana was enough to wreck everything those few happy moments with Eduardo had achieved, and she almost wept as she signalled Eric to silence while she answered for him.

'Señor Truman exaggerates, as he told you,' she insisted in a voice that she found impossible to steady. 'In fact I met him for the first time when he gatecrashed our wedding reception. He's very simply a neighbour; not even a friend, only a passing acquaintance!'

Hurtful or not, she hoped to put Eric Truman firmly in his place, and at the same time put paid to any ideas that Juana might have, providing she was believed, of course. 'Really?' Juana smiled.

'Actually,' Lari stressed, 'he was on the point of leaving when you arrived.' In fact she had an aching desire to be rid of both of them and protocol went by the book as she sought to send Juana packing too. 'I didn't expect to see you either, *señora*; had you any special reason for coming?'

Her challenge brought no more than a mocking smile, and Lari guessed it would take more than that to outface Juana Cortez. 'I came to see how the workmen are getting along with the house,' Juana told her, 'but since you are here I need not stay. I shall see you back at Santa Inés, Lari, Señor Truman, I am pleased to have met you; *adios*!' She turned and was making for the door before Lari could say another word, pausing in the doorway to look back. 'I shall tell Eduardo that all is going well,' she promised. '*Adios!*'

'Wait!'

Whatever either of them thought of her, Lari was anxious to do what she could to retrieve the situation. Inevitably Juana meant to pass on what she had seen to Eduardo, and however hard it was to bring herself to the point of appealing to her Lari saw herself with little choice but to try.

The other woman stood in the doorway, and her half-smile was enough to confirm Lari's worst fears, for it mocked her anxiety and anticipated her appeal with relish. Just for a moment Lari was tempted by the idea of slapping that smooth smiling face as hard as she could, but if she had the position would have been irretrievable. Instead she steeled herself to pleading, however hard it was.

'You—you said something about seeing Eduardo,' she began, and Juana nodded, still smiling but saying nothing. 'I just wanted to say that there's no need for you to tell him about——' She glanced over her shoulder at Eric Truman's disconsolate figure in the hall. 'I'm seeing him myself at lunchtime, he's taking me into Seville——'

'You're lunching with him?'

That had been a mistake, Lari realised; the idea of an intimate lunch for two would do nothing to appease those malicious dark eyes that glared resentment at her. Lari knew her cause was lost, but she nevertheless pressed on, though with even less optimism than before. 'I just wanted to say that it would be better—I'd rather you left it to me to tell him about—this.'

'Oh, I'm sure you would!'

'Not that there's anything at all underhand,' Lari pressed on desperately, 'but Eduardo might not understand——'

'I'm not sure I understand it,' Juana declared coolly. 'He's quite an attractive man, but you're a fool to play around when you have someone like Eduardo.' Her near-black eyes glowed malice as she thrust out her lower lip derisively. 'But of course yours isn't really a marriage, is it?' Her sudden laughter stung like a lash and Lari flinched from it as she watched the woman she had so often suspected was her husband's lover turn and walk away. 'I can imagine how you must feel knowing you're only a means to an end,' she taunted as she got into her car, 'and believe me I'm sorry for you! *Adios*, Lari; or should I say *hasta luego*, because I'll be seeing you later, won't I?'

She closed the car door and started the engine, turning to wave a mocking hand before she drove off towards the *bodegas*. And as she watched her go Lari knew that as long as she lived she would never hate anyone as much as she did Juana Cortez at that moment.

Instead of waiting in happy anticipation for Eduardo to take her to lunch, Lari was anxious and plainly unhappy, so that Marta in her wisdom said little, keeping her own counsel as to the cause. Eric Truman had left immediately after Juana, and Lari made no secret of the fact that she was glad to see him go, for she half expected that Eduardo would come to see for himself whether or not she was entertaining the man he had so clearly mistrusted.

It was almost two o'clock, however, before she heard another car stop outside and her heart was pounding hard as she got instinctively to her feet, while Marta discreetly made herself scarce, turning in the doorway to offer a word of advice. 'Smile a little, *señora*, eh?' she suggested softly, but Lari found it much harder than she would have believed possible.

The familiar heavy tread came quickly across the hall, and she sat on the edge of the kitchen table as the door opened and Eduardo came in. She looked small and solitary in the centre of the big kitchen surrounded by the unfamiliar setting of pots and pans and scrubbed kitchen furniture, and Eduardo paused for a moment in the doorway. Then catching her anxious eye, he held it steadily.

'I'm glad to find you alone,' he said, and Lari's senses responded with mingled regret and bitterness.

Her colour was high and the tears she had expected to shed were banished by the familiar thrill of battle. Why should she cry over him? He had probably spent far more of the morning with Juana Cortez than she had with Eric, and what was good enough for one was good enough for the other; so she told herself as she faced him. Nevertheless she glanced upward with a hint of uncertainty before she replied.

'Obviously you've seen Juana Cortez!'

'You know I have,' he replied shortly, 'since Juana herself told you. And for your information I don't enjoy hearing that my wife is entertaining her lover in our home while I'm otherwise occupied! Please—don't bother to deny it, for how else could he have known you'd be here this morning, if you didn't arrange to see him? Damn it, Lari, why did you do it?' She found it incredibly hard to meet his eyes, and yet she still could not allow that he was any more entitled to act like an outraged spouse than she was. 'You swore to me that you had no ulterior motive for coming with me this morning,' he went on, 'and yet the minute my back is turned your lover is here!'

'He's *not* my lover!' Her eyes gleamed darkly and her cheeks were flushed, for he had not, she realised, even attempted to deny that Juana Cortez had been with him. 'And if he was,' she pressed on recklessly, 'I don't see that you can make a fuss about it when Juana Cortez comes sneaking down to see you everyday!'

His eyes narrowed to slits and one hand was already raised threateningly when Marta first tapped lightly on the kitchen door and then came in. The ensuing silence was fraught with turbulence and Lari was shivering when she eventually drew her eyes away from the hand that now brushed forcefully through his thick black hair.

If Marta realised what she had interrupted, her expression gave no hint of it as she glanced from one to the other. 'Excuse me, *señor*,' she said, 'but are you and the *señora* still going out for lunch, or can I prepare something for you?'

'Oh no, Marta, thank you, that won't be necessary. Only a faint huskiness betrayed how close he had come to losing control, and when he looked down at Lari she found it impossible to read what was in his eyes. 'If you're ready to leave,' he said, 'we'll go now.'

Lari was uncertain of him and of his mood, for she had quite expected he would not even bother to come for her at all after waiting so long. The tight line of his mouth was hardly encouraging, but she could see no reason not to go with him if he was still prepared to keep their lunch date, and she nodded consent as she reached for her handbag. 'I'm ready,' she said.

They crossed the hall in silence with Marta immediately behind them, and in the doorway Lari turned and gave her a faint smile. Marta's dark face was solemn and she merely inclined her head, her black eyes deep with warning as she saw them off, and via the driving mirror, as they drove off, Lari saw her cross herself before going back into the house.

The drive into Seville was made mostly in silence, and they were coming into the suburban outskirts when Lari ventured to mention the incident that had been troubling her ever since it happened. Glancing at Eduardo's shadowed face, she chose a moment when he needed to keep his eyes on the road before she spoke.

'Would you really have—hit me, Eduardo?' she asked in a very small voice, and for a moment he appeared too preoccupied with the traffic to answer her.

'I'd have been very sorry if I had,' he said eventually, 'and I don't really think I could actually have struck you, however provoked I was.' He turned his head brefly while they were stopped at an intersection, and his eyes were still unfathomable so that she was no wiser as to what he might be thinking. 'Do you believe I could, Lari?'

She didn't honestly know, although she felt he would have been acting very much out of character if he had actually struck her, and she shook her head. 'You were always such a gentle man,' she told him. 'I remember that's what I loved—liked most about you when I was a little girl.'

Eduardo laughed shortly, and shook his head. 'How much simpler it would be if you were *still* a little girl!' he declared. 'I find it hard to realise you're not, Lari, and when you provoke me as you did this morning I feel—confused and uncertain how I should treat you. I have Anchoterrias because I promised to care for you as Tío José wished me to, and I must never forget that promise, whether or not it was made to Tío José personally.' He turned his head again briefly and his eyes showed a glimmer of the old warmth. 'I promise not to forget again, Lari.'

'Eduardo——'

'Now may we forget the matter,' he interrupted quickly when she would have told him how far out in his estimation of what caring for her meant to her. 'I find too serious conversation interferes with my enjoyment of lunch.'

Thankful that he wasn't bent on spending the next hour and a half lecturing her about Eric Truman, Lari readily agreed. 'I wondered if you'd come for me after all,' she said. 'I'm glad you did.'

Again he spared her a brief glance, but in this instance, she noted, there was a faintly sardonic smile on his mouth. 'Naturally I came for you,' he told her. 'I don't propose starving you to death in addition to my other shortcomings as a husband.'

'Oh, but I didn't——'

'And since you seem intent on discussing the matter,' Eduardo went on as if she had not spoken, 'I promised that nothing would change when you married me, and as far as possible I shall keep my word on that. Just as long as you keep things within the bounds of reason and don't cause gossip, you may do as you wish, I shan't interfere. That—incident this morning was *not* discreet, Lari, and I think you must allow that I had cause for objection. Secret meetings with Eric Truman aren't reasonable or discreet. I realise it must be hard for you when all you want to do is live your life in the way you like best, but——'

He spread a hand in a gesture of apology, and Lari wondered how he could possibly know her so little. Somehow he had got hold of the idea that all she expected of him was that he would allow her to go her own way and continue to treat her with the same gentle kindness he had shown her as a child, and until she was much more sure of his situation with Juana Cortez she felt hesitant about letting him know how wrong he was.

'Now,' he said as he drove the car along a wide avenue lined with orange trees, 'shall we agree not to mention either your misdemeanours or mine—at least until after we've had lunch?'

Lari nodded ready acceptance, and by the time they had reached the coffee stage of their substantial meal she was feeling much more relaxed. She enjoyed the sensation of eating in a public place with a man as attractive as Eduardo, and he was an attentive companion so that she responded readily to his mood. Smiling, she listened to him talk about everything under the sun except the controversial subject of their relationship, and that was not even mentioned.

Her more relaxed mood had its effect on the way she looked too, and without her realising it the soft curve of her mouth became almost sensual whenever she smiled or laughed, and her cheeks were flushed. Only her eyes, carefully shielded by the downward sweep of lashes, could have given away her innermost feelings, and she was careful to keep those from him.

As he sat with his elbows resting on the table in front of him, he was that much closer, and the big brown hands that held his coffee cup were a reminder of that earlier threat of violence that had so surprised her. She had never associated physical violence with Eduardo, and she had to believe him when he said he could not have brought himself to the point of striking her, no matter how provoked he was.

Nevertheless she felt that there were depths to his character that she had not yet discovered, and it was the strange mixture of gentleness and ruthlessness that made him such a fascinating man. She could even understand Juana Cortez's fury at losing him, though she couldn't condone her spite. How much more spiteful would she have been if she had known about that stunningly unexpected kiss just before they parted? she wondered.

Remembering that, Lari looked up and found Eduardo studying her with such a thoughtful expression that she tilted her head to one side and smiled at him curiously. 'What are you thinking about?' she asked, and he put down his cup carefully. 'You look—unsure about something.'

He looked so serious that just for a moment her heart fluttered anxiously. 'You're very astute,' he told her, 'and I don't quite know how to tell you what I have to in the circumstances.'

Her stomach seemed to be filled with fluttering and a chill crept over her skin as she looked at him, her eyes anxious and appealing. 'Eduardo? What—are you trying to say?'

'That I had forgotten how you feel about the *corrida.*'

Lari's reactions were mixed. She disliked the bullfights, but if he had arranged to take her to one she would go uncomplainingly, simply because he was taking her, but again she kept her eyes hidden while she answered him. 'I don't much like it,' she said, choosing her words carefully, 'but I'll come with you if you've booked us seats, Eduardo.'

'Seats have been booked, including one for you.' He

too seemed to be choosing his words and she was frowning at him curiously. 'In fact I've been persuaded to appear next week at the local *corrida* to celebrate the Feast of Santa Inés. Madre committed me to it, and it is a matter of pride for them, of course, that I appear.'

Lari felt physically sick, but not for anything would she have let him see it, for it was as he said, a matter of pride to his family that he was a talented amateur *torero* with a reputation for courage. She could not bear to think of him risking injury and possibly worse simply for the sake of exhibiting his skill with the sword and *muleta*, but her in-laws, without exception, would never understand her squeamishness, and she had to accept it or widen the gap between them.

Lari swallowed hard, bringing her revulsion under control. 'Of course you can't let them down,' she told him, but her expression and the tone of her voice left him in little doubt about her own feelings, and he reached out a hand, pressing his long gentle fingers over hers.

'I would like you to be there, Lari.'

She found it hard to agree without saying anything about her own reaction, and yet if she did it could mean losing any ground she might have gained, and she couldn't face that. Juana Cortez would almost certainly be at the *corrida*, and Juana already had too many advantages.

'I'll be there,' she promised, and prayed she wouldn't disgrace herself or him when it came to the point. 'I promise I'll be there, Eduardo.'

'Chica!' Eduardo said softly, and Lari remembered him using that same endearment often when she first knew him. Nothing had changed, it seemed.

CHAPTER SIX

THE excitement of fiesta preparations took precedence over almost everything else, but Lari would have looked forward to it with much more enthusiasm had it not been for the part Eduardo was to play in the celebratory *corrida* at the local bullring. She was the only member of the family who did not anticipate the event with pride and pleasure, and though she realised that her attitude did nothing to improve relations between her and her formidable mother-in-law, she couldn't pretend to feel something she didn't.

She wished it was possible to persuade Eduardo not to take part, but although their relationship had improved during the last few days, she did not feel capable of persuading him against something that both he and his family looked forward to so excitedly.

He was on her mind when she left her bedroom one morning, and when she caught sight of him walking away from her along the landing, she almost called out to him. It was only because she sensed a certain air of purpose about him that she kept quiet, but she watched him for a moment, curious about his destination. Their bedrooms were divided by a shower that only he used, and the stairs lay in the opposite direction, so he wasn't making his way downstairs.

Wrapped in a red silk dressing-robe and with his hands in the pockets, he still somehow managed to look impressive, and somehow it was irresistible to stay long enough to see where in fact he went. Striding soft-footed along the carpeted gallery, he came to a halt suddenly outside one of the bedroom doors, and when she realised whose room it was, Lari caught her breath and went hurrying across and into the more conventional bathroom opposite, hoping he hadn't seen her.

She was shaking like a leaf as she leaned against the bathroom door for a moment, trying to control an impulse she had to pound with her fists on the wooden panels in sheer frustration at her own weakness.

It was something she should have expected, something she had thought she already accepted, but somehow the hurt was no less because of it, and she despaired of her own vulnerability where Eduardo was concerned. Juana Cortez wasn't a woman to give up easily, and Eduardo would surely find her much more to his taste than a young and very inexperienced wife. Nor was it a new situation, for Marta had told her about their earlier relationship, and they had been lovers long before Eduardo knew that he would have to marry Lari before he could inherit Anchoterrias.

She took her bath automatically, her thoughts chaotic, so that when she eventually emerged from the bathroom it was in a mood of mingled anger and misery, and she vowed that never again would she allow herself to be lulled into acceptance by her dangerously attractive husband. If he wanted Juana Cortez, he could have her, but Lari would go her own way, and she would never again cry over him.

Vaguely aware of someone approaching, she turned swiftly, half afraid it might be Eduardo returning to his own room, and she felt the cold thrill of hate when she saw who it was come hurrying along the gallery. Juana Cortez had never looked more sleek and smooth and feline, as she advanced too quickly to make escape possible, and she regarded Lari's glistening and tear-stained eyes with speculative interest. Nor did she miss the swift glance Lari gave along the gallery towards the door at which she had seen Eduardo pause before going in.

'Is something wrong?' she asked, dark eyes gleaming, and Lari shook her head.

'No, nothing's wrong, *señora*.'

'You can never bring yourself to call me Juana, can you?'

The dark eyes mocked her, knowing her reasons well enough. She was wearing a dress of beige-coloured silk that fitted her flatteringly close, and her black hair gleamed in the sunshine from a high window, glossy as sable. She was a stunningly sensual woman and no one was more aware of it than Juana herself; a woman who, Lari was forced to recognise, would be a fit partner for Eduardo's fierce passion.

'You've been crying,' she observed, and evidently found it of interest, for she was smiling with her blood-red mouth. 'Has something upset you, Lari? Or some-*one*, maybe?'

'I'm perfectly O.K., thank you,' Lari murmured, hating the shaky uncertainty of her voice. 'But I'd better get dressed, or I'll be late for breakfast.'

'Oh, there's no rush,' Juana assured her, and caught her reluctant gaze, holding it boldly while she went on. 'Eduardo isn't dressed yet, so you've plenty of time.'

It was impossible to mistake her meaning, and Lari's pulse hammered mercilessly as she fought for control of her tangled emotions. It took every ounce of self-control she had not to hit out as temptation urged her to. 'Nevertheless, I don't like to be too late, so if you'll excuse me, *señora*——'

She broke off when long hard fingers gripped her jaw and turned her face so that Juana could look into it. 'You saw him come to my room, didn't you?' she asked softly, and watched the swift flush of colour in Lari's cheeks. Then she laughed and thrust her away, brushing away Lari's vague gestures of repulsion. 'Well, now you know!'

In the brief tussle Lari dropped the packet of make-up tissues she was carrying, and she bent to retrieve them automatically when they landed at Juana's feet. It was as she started to straighten up again that she caught sight of something that held her poised for a full five seconds, staring in startled realisation. For across one slim ankle ran a thin white scar, clear and unmistakable, and Lari was remembering another occasion on which she had seen an exactly similar blemish.

There could be no doubt, it did not even enter her mind to admit a coincidence, that slender ankle with its barely discernible scar was the same one she had noticed first when she was trapped in the lift of a Seville store. Only on that occasion the slim elegant feet had been wearing expensive crocodile shoes; the kind she had seen Juana wearing the day she met her at the *bodegas*, on her way to see Eduardo.

Lari stood up slowly and her heart thudded wildly as she stared into those huge and menacing black eyes. She dared not let Juana even guess what made her appear so startled suddenly, but she had absolutely no doubt at all now that the warning notice had been removed from the lift deliberately—if not with the intention of killing her, at least of causing her injury, and certainly to frighten her.

Numb with shock, she murmured something inaudible that Juana Cortez took for an excuse, then turned into her room, but somehow those dark malicious eyes stayed fixed immovably in her mind's eye. What she took for hate in her own feelings was nothing like the deep, chilling emotion that motivated the other woman, and Lari was suddenly very much afraid.

Lari's choice of someone to confide in about her fears was limited, and how was she to convince Eduardo that the woman he had practically admitted was his lover had been the person responsible for what could have been a fatal accident? It did not even enter her head that he might have been a party to it, for whatever his shortcomings she could not see him in that light at all.

For the rest of the day she kept to herself as far as possible, and avoided Juana Cortez altogether, while she awaited Eduardo's return in the evening. Even then, as the seemingly interminable evening wore on she began to think there would never be an opportunity to see him alone. In fact it seemed almost as if he might have suspected her need, for the rest had already retired and still he lingered, looking across at her for a moment before coming across to join her where she stood by one of the windows.

She sought the reassurance of his gently enquiring look, and yet when he placed a light hand on her cheek she instinctively drew away from it. He frowned, though he still stood facing her, sensitive to her need, it seemed. 'What's wrong, Lari?'

The deep voice had its inevitable effect and made it so much harder for her, so that she shook her head. 'I—I don't quite know where to begin,' she confessed, and he smiled faintly, though his eyes were serious.

'Is it so difficult?' he asked. He didn't attempt to touch her again and Lari already regretted that impulsive rejection, born of seeing him on his way to Juana Cortez. 'What can be troubling you enough to make you look like a little ghost?' His dark eyes scanned her face, but it was impossible to guess what he was thinking. 'If I can't comfort you,' he went on, 'at least tell me what's making you so unhappy.'

It seemed an almost automatic gesture when he reached out to her again, and this time Lari did not reject him, but accepted the clasp of his strong fingers gratefully. 'I haven't anyone else I can tell, and I——'

'Who else *would* you tell but me?' Eduardo demanded, and when he drew her closer to him, his vibrance made her shiver. Steering her in to the corner of the *salón*, he perched himself on the very edge of an armchair and sat her down in one facing him, still holding her hands. 'I'm listening,' he promised, and Lari's heart fluttered anxiously.

Looking down at their clasped hands, she tried to bring order to her churning emotions, and found it even harder to begin than she had anticipated. 'I-it's about that accident I had in the lift, just before we were married,' she ventured, and a brief upward glance showed a barely perceptible tightening of his mouth. 'I know you said I was imagining part of it, Eduardo,' she went on, oddly anxious to convince him, 'but you'll see I was right about one thing at least. There was a woman—you remember I told you she was standing right by the lift when it dropped the first time and I asked her to go for help? You said—the manager said, there wasn't anyone, but I know there was.'

His eyes were narrowed, and Lari's heart pounded anxiously. If he turned from her now, she didn't know what she would do. 'Lari, why all this again now? So long afterwards.'

'Because you still think I was imagining it!' she insisted, 'and I wasn't, Eduardo!' Looking up again, her eyes reproached him. 'You promised to listen,' she said, and caught her breath when he leaned across and kissed her.

'I'll listen,' he promised soothingly, 'but I still can't think why you're letting that business still worry you. It's all over and done with.'

'But it isn't!' He looked at her sharply, and Lari flicked an anxious tongue over her lips before she went on. 'Oh, please, let me explain, Eduardo; I want—I *need* to tell someone!'

He was obviously concerned about her nervousness, and yet she knew he wasn't going to be easily convinced. 'Very well,' he said quietly, 'I promised.'

She clung to his strong fingers thankfully and hurried on, for he would probably withdraw that comforting clasp all too soon now. 'As I told you,' she went on, 'I could see the woman from the knees down, her feet were at eye level, and I called to her, asked her to get help, and I'm sure she heard me. There was something —I don't know, something about the way she stood.' He nodded, as if he understood what she meant, and she hurried on, anxious to have it over. 'I told you she was wearing crocodile-skin shoes, but that wasn't all—there was a small thin white scar running diagonally across her left ankle, I saw it quite distinctly.'

Eduardo said nothing for the moment, but the hands that held hers were withdrawn to clasp together tightly between his knees, and thick lashes came down to hide whatever was in his eyes. Lari thought she knew the signs and she waited, shivering with anticipation of the fury she felt sure must come soon.

Instead, when he spoke again his voice was quiet and steady, and there was only a hint of harshness to betray how he was feeling. 'And when did you discover that Juana has a scar on her left ankle?' he asked.

Lari's head jerked upward, suspecting his tone, ready for his anger and scarcely believing his present quietness. 'I—I met her on the gallery this morning, and I dropped my tissues; when I bent to pick——'

'You quarrelled?'

He asked it so quietly, yet managed to suggest that it was because of what had happened between them that she had seen fit to raise the matter of the incident in the lift again. 'Not exactly,' she denied. 'But she seemed to know that I'd seen you——'

She stopped herself quickly, biting on her lip and hastily avoiding narrowed dark eyes. 'Seen me—what, Lari?'

'It—it doesn't matter!'

'Oh, but I think it does!' He got to his feet and stood with his back to her and she could see the taut anger in him as she gnawed at her lower lip. Swinging round suddenly, he frowned down at her, his dark eyes fierce and angry. 'You didn't mention a scar at the time, and now suddenly, because Juana says something to upset you, you claim the woman, whom no one else saw, had a scar on her ankle!'

'She did, and so has Juana! She also wears crocodile shoes!'

'Mother of God!' Eduardo swore. 'Half the woman in Spain have a pair of crocodile shoes; it's no reason for suggesting—Holy Mother, do you realise *what* you're implying?'

'I saw her; I saw the woman by the lift and I saw the same scar on Juana Cortez's ankle, you can't deny it's there!'

'I *don't* deny it's there!'

'But it wasn't because I saw you going to her room, and she knew I'd seen you and couldn't resist—goading me about it! I didn't mention it before because you didn't give me the opportunity, but I *did* see the scar that day, and—I know it's the same.'

Her voice tapered off when she realised the way he was looking at her, although she did not for the moment understand why he looked as he did. 'Oh, Lari!' He reached down and took her hands again, drawing her to her feet. His voice was barely above a whisper, and something gleamed in his eyes that touched her senses without her being aware of it. 'Lari, my dear, sweet, suspicious child—so that's it! I'd collected the mail, my dear, and there was a letter for Juana about a new *capataz* she's been pestering me to find for her. I thought she'd want to have it, so I took it along for her, that's all.'

She wanted to believe it, she believed it in her heart even if her senses cautioned her, but it didn't make any difference to the fact of Juana Cortez having the identical scar that the woman by the lift had had, even so. 'I—I didn't know,' she whispered. 'I saw you go to her door, and when I saw her afterwards, she——'

'Juana is a bitch,' he stated matter-of-factly, and when she looked up he was smiling a little wryly. 'She's beautiful and sexy, but she's a bitch, and I know you've come in for more than your share.'

'Eduardo, I did see her there; I know it was her by the lift and she—she didn't get help when I asked her to.'

'Lari, please, little one, don't frighten yourself like this!'

'But I *am* frightened,' she insisted. 'I admit that I don't like her, but it's more than that and I can't—I'm scared to death whether or not it makes sense, and I don't know what to do! I want—I need your help, Eduardo, please!'

If only she could bring herself to believe wholeheartedly his version of why he had been visiting Juana's room. Juana's own account so closely matched her own original suspicion that it was hard to reject it out of hand, however passionately she wanted to.

Eduardo sighed and reached out, running long gentle fingers down her cheek, then sliding them under her hair and drawing her to him until she was pressed close to the warm reassuring strength of him. He laid his face lightly on the softness of her hair while his other arm clasped her tightly as they stood in silence for a moment.

'Oh, Lari,' he breathed, 'what am I going to do about you?'

Receiving no answer, he cradled the back of her head in one big hand and tipped it so that he could look down into her face, and she noticed a small and disturbingly enigmatic smile on his mouth that may or may not have shown in his eyes, she couldn't be sure.

Then he bent and kissed her mouth, not fiercely but lightly and gently, while his left arm completely enfolded her and its hand spanned with intimate persuasion over the softness of her breast.

'Nothing and no one is going to hurt you, Lari, you've nothing to feel frightened about. And if you need me to comfort you, you don't need to plead so anxiously with me as if you think I'll turn you away. Haven't I promised to take care of you? Do you still not accept that I'll always be here when you need me?'

Desperately Lari clung to him, and her fear was already retreating before other more pressing emotions that his nearness aroused. 'I *do* need you,' she whispered. 'You don't *know* how I need you!'

'Because you're afraid, Lari?'

He spoke in the deep and seductively warm voice that could always affect her so deeply, and she shook her head. With one hand he brushed the hair back from her forehead, a light evocative touch that affected every nerve in her body, and kissed her forehead, a mere brush of his lips and incredibly tantalising.

'Eduardo——' Her eyes when she looked up at him had none of the dark haunted look that had drawn his sympathy in the first place; they were wide and bright and they met his only briefly. 'Not—not only because I'm afraid,' she whispered, and he kissed her again, then repeated the light, evocative caress over and over until she closed her eyes and sought to prolong it into something more positive.

'Go to bed, little one,' he murmured with his mouth close to her ear so that his breath warmed her neck and she shivered with pleasure. 'Go to bed and trust me to see that you have no more cause to be frightened; will you? Will you let me care for you as I've always wanted to, little one? I want you to go to bed now—and trust me, hmm?'

It wasn't the moment to leave him, and she didn't

need his promise to care for her. It was what she had asked for, but it wasn't all she wanted or had hoped for, yet she nodded agreement, and he was easing her away from him, kissing her mouth and her softly flushed cheeks. She stood for a moment with her head bowed and her eyes hidden by their lashes, and her body throbbed with a need of him that was far more urgent than anything she had known before.

'I trust you,' she whispered huskily, and again lifted her face to him, her lips parted and trembling with eagerness for his kiss. 'Goodnight, Eduardo.'

He pressed his mouth slowly over hers and its pressure increased until she felt every nerve in her body responding, then he lifted his head, his lips clinging for as long as possible, and lingering even while he spoke. 'Go to bed, Lari,' he murmured, and briefly renewed the pressure of his mouth. 'And please—don't be frightened.'

Lari had never before left him so reluctantly, and her whole being rebelled at the very idea of his sending her off to her solitary bed. With that in mind she gave him a last appealing look before he turned her about and sent her towards the door, and she walked on legs that were alarmingly unsteady. She paused in the doorway to hear his whispered 'goodnight', then reached for the door half open behind her.

Upstairs in her room she found it impossible to even consider sleeping, and she stood by the window looking out at the moonlit landscape, and trying to come to terms with the tangle of emotions Eduardo had aroused in her. It wasn't Anchoterrias, but the landscape was very much the same and she had a sudden longing for the familiarity of the old house amid its dark sea of vines, jewelled with silver ribbons where the irrigation channels reflected the moonlight and wound endlessly downward. Her home and Eduardo were all she needed, all she would ever need, but she could be certain of only one of them, and she knew as she stood there watching the moonlit landscape that it was the least important of the two.

She had no idea how long she had stood there when she heard a faint sound behind her like a latch clicking and turned swiftly, her eyes darting across the room to the door into the adjoining shower room. Another similar door gave Eduardo access from his side, but he had never so far taken advantage of the fact to come through to her, and as she saw him there, tall and darkly shadowed, Lari's breathing became suddenly more deep and laboured and more audible.

She watched him come slowly across the room, but the bedside lamp gave little light and it was difficult to see what his expression was, but even in that moment of startled disbelief she noticed that he was wearing the same red silk robe he had been wearing that morning when she saw him on the gallery. Just for a moment her pride rebelled at the thought of her own situation being merely a repetition of that earlier one with Juana Cortez, but he had explained that and her heart chose to believe it whatever her common sense told her.

She had not dared hope that he meant to come to her, and as she stood by the window still, she was shivering with an inner excitement she had never known before. Lean and soft-footed, he came slowly towards her and she could see the faint smile that curved his mouth and gleamed in the darkness of his eyes.

'Aren't you in bed yet?' The words were mundane enough, but the voice that spoke them was barely above a whisper, and it drew her like a lure, seducing her senses and drawing her across the room towards him. 'Lari?'

They came face to face at the foot of the bed and her heart was beating so hard that it stunned her with its violence, so that she passed her tongue slowly across her lips while she watched his face with a fascination that was almost hypnotic. He looked down into her small flushed face and then briefly across at the lamp burning beside the bed; a couple of steps and the lamp snicked off, plunging them suddenly into the pale soft shimmer of moonlight.

'Weren't you expecting me?' A hand raised her face to him and in the brief moment when she raised her own eyes she saw the glowing darkness of his and shivered. 'Oh, Lari; little one!'

He held her close, his arms pressing her to the virile warmth of bronzed flesh while his hands stroked over her back, moving caressingly slowly around under her arms and over the soft contours her dress revealed. He bent his head and pressed his lips to the nape of her neck, his face buried in the silky paleness of her hair, murmuring things she scarcely heard for the wild thudding of her heart.

'I thought you'd be waiting for me,' he whispered. 'Instead you're still dressed and——' He kissed her neck and nuzzled the soft skin below her ear while he spoke. 'Lari, you don't mean to send me away, do you?'

She could no more send him away at that moment than she could have surrendered her life, and there was a fine arrogance in his voice that suggested he knew it. Still she had no will to speak, so she merely shook her head, wisping her fine hair over his face and muffling his voice.

'Let me help you, hmm?'

His voice caressed her senses and she stood silent and waiting, submitting to his every wish because she seemed not to be able to help herself. His hands slid down her back, drawing her against him, and he felt tense and vibrant, his eyes as they looked down into hers, gleaming and black as polished jet in the moonlight.

He handled her deftly and surely and incredibly gently, his arms holding her captive while his hands slid open the zip in the back of her dress, his long fingers evoking shivers of pleasure as they slipped along her spine. He let her go only briefly while her dress dropped to the floor and at once her skin was touched by his warmth, a closer and much more intimate warmth than she had ever known before, sensitive to the brush of dark hair in the careless opening of his robe.

His arms enclosed her again and she shivered in anticipation of their strength. One by one light flimsy garments fluttered like pale silent moths to the floor, and her softness was drawn closer still, moulded firmly to the lean vigour of his body and yielding quite independently of the sounds that issued from her lips in the moment before he silenced her.

Vaguely she felt it was like being drowned, for his arms held her relentlessly firm, submerging her in a tide of violent excitement until she could no longer breathe except by way of the mouth that possessed hers. A hard, searching mouth that sought to conquer and subdue, yet gentle too when her lips parted and yielded in response.

No longer conscious of anything but her need for him, she was trembling and eager as she lifted her arms to encircle his neck, while her body responded wantonly to the muscular strength that strained her to him. Lifting her into his arms, he carried her to the bed and laid her down on it, keeping his hold on her still, and Lari stirred, seeking even closer contact, to become one with the virile force that sought her surrender.

'My love!' she whispered against his mouth.

Her hands curled, tight-fingered, into his thick black hair and she murmured against the possessive mouth, small soft sounds of sheer pleasure. Nothing mattered except that she had at last become Eduardo's wife in more than name, and it was as joyous and exciting as she had always dreamed. Juana Cortez had never been further from her mind.

It was quite a bit later than usual when Lari woke the following morning, and she lay for a moment or two savouring a sensation of utter and complete contentment. Never in her life before did she remember feeling as she did then, and she stretched out an arm to the pillow beside her and found the indent of another head in the soft downy cushion that reminded her.

Rolling on to her front, she buried her face in the hollow, and stretched her body in the sheer sensual enjoyment of recollection. Then equally swiftly she twisted right over on to her back and gazed for a moment at the bathroom door that stood partly open, her eyes bright and heavy-lidded as she listened to sounds of the shower being turned off.

'Eduardo?'

A brief silence followed, then his head appeared around the edge of the door, his hair tousled and still wet. His tanned face gleaming and freshly shaven smiled at her and the red silk robe clung to a still damp torso. 'Who else?' he demanded, and she laughed, throwing out her arms to him.

It was a blatant invitation, and one he obviously did not like to refuse, for he came and stood beside the bed, taking her hand and stroking his long fingers caressingly up and down her inner arm. 'I'm already late,' he told her. 'I can't let you tempt me, my lovely, although I find you very hard to resist. There were so many things I wanted to say to you too, but——' He stroked a forefinger down the length of her body where it was outlined by the covers, and laughed softly. 'You slept so long, my baby, that they will have to wait until another time. But oh, you tempt me!'

'Do I?'

Lari held tightly to his hand and he dropped on to

the edge of the bed; flirting with Eduardo was a new experience and she was enjoying it. He slipped his arms underneath her while his weight pinned her firmly on to the bed and his mouth was deliberately forceful when he kissed her.

'You know you do,' he told her in a voice that was slightly husky and shiveringly deep. 'But I have to dress and be in the practice ring by ten, my love, and I'm getting later every minute I stay here with you!'

To Lari nothing existed this morning but her love for him, and the reminder that he was to fight in the *corrida* in two days' time was doubly unwelcome in the circumstances. She hugged closer suddenly and pressed her face to the warmth of olive dark skin, her eyes closed and willing herself not to plead with him.

'Eduardo, oh, my love!'

He held her close for a moment, then raised himself and kissed her cheek, his hands on her shoulders and making a moue of regret for his own insistence. 'I know you hate it, *amada*,' he murmured, while his thumbs caressed her shoulders, 'but I'm committed and I couldn't get out of it even if I wanted to.'

Lari speculated, watching him through her long lashes, and her mouth was slightly pursed. 'And you don't want to,' she guessed, knowing it was true.

'I don't want to.'

As always he was straightforward about it, and gave her no false hope that his new love for her would allow her to influence his decision. To Lari the thought of him being exposed to possible serious injury, even death, had no excitement at all and she was silent, with her eyes downcast and her hands placed flat-palmed on his chest.

'Shall—shall I come down to the practice ring with you, Eduardo? I will if you want me to; if you'd like me to, even though I don't like it and I'd be terrified every minute you were in there.'

He placed his hands either side of her face and studied its soft flushed cheeks for a moment in silence, then he bent and kissed her mouth, gently and lingeringly and for a very long time. 'I know you don't want to come, my little one,' he murmured against her lips, 'and I don't want you to do anything that makes you unhappy. All I ask is that you come to the *corrida* on Sunday.'

'I promised I would,' she reminded him, and again Eduardo leaned to kiss her.

'Then I won't expect you to watch practice as well.' He smiled into her eyes and the look in his dark ones brought a hard urgent thudding to her heart. 'And now I *must* go or I shall be keeping all sorts of people waiting and destroy my reputation for being punctual.' He stroked a finger down the length of her small and slightly upturned nose before kissing its tip lightly. 'And you'd better get up or Madre will think you're not coming down to breakfast this morning. I shan't have time for any if I'm going to be on time.'

'Oh, but you——'

'Sssh!' he commanded, and bent to kiss her before he turned away. 'I'll see you later, eh?'

Lari watched him as far as the bathroom door, then flung back the covers, startled for a moment by the sight of her own complete nakedness. She had never felt less inhibited in her life, and when she surveyed her reflection in the long bathroom mirror a few minutes later she no longer saw a naïve girl longing for her husband's love, but a woman fulfilled. Eduardo loved her, he had proved it very thoroughly last night, and nothing could take that from her. The fears of last night were firmly pushed to the back of her mind, overtaken by newer and more important sensations.

She sang to herself all the time she was bathing, and afterwards as she revelled in the luxury of scenting her body with some rather special perfume she had bought before her wedding. Eduardo wouldn't be spending all day in the practice ring, and when he came home——She was smiling when she opened her bedroom door shortly afterwards, and she walked along the gallery to the stairs feeling as she never had before.

As she started downstairs the sound of a woman's laughter reached her and she turned her head swiftly in the direction of it, looking over the high balustrade into the hall. She had no doubt who it was who laughed and just for a second Juana Cortez again intruded into her contentment. She had barely time to dismiss the feeling when the woman herself came into view, appearing from below the curving staircase, and much too preoccupied to notice Lari up there at the top of the stairs.

Wearing black trousers that fitted her to perfection, and a flame-coloured silk shirt, she smiled confidently up at her companion, her arm linked closely with his. It was impossible for Lari to see his face from her vantage point, but as they walked side by side to the door, those fine dark eyes again beamed appreciation at him when he held it open for her. Seeing them leave the house together like that, it took very little effort on Lari's part to understand why Eduardo had dissuaded her from visiting the practice ring with him, and she closed her eyes as she pressed both hands to her mouth to quell the small hurt sound that sought to escape.

Lari spent most of the morning on the *patio* reading, or seeming to read, a magazine, but in reality her mind was in a chaos of indecision. She had even considered the step of leaving there and then and never going back to Anchoterrias, for she could not easily see herself settling into the same routine again after last night.

It had been bad enough before, but now that she

knew what loving him could be like, she couldn't ever face sharing him with Juana Cortez. Now that he had Anchoterrias he surely wouldn't try too hard to make her go back with him, and he could even have Juana move in if that was what he wanted. Although she doubted very much if he would retain Marta's services for very long, if she did.

By lunch time she was no nearer to a solution, and she carefully avoided Eduardo as much as was possible, though it wasn't easy, and the familiar frown followed her refusal to walk out on to the *patio* with him. 'What's wrong, Lari?' he asked, quietly because he was as aware as she was of his mother's interested gaze. 'What's happened since I left you this morning?' The temptation was to blurt it out there and then regardless of who would hear her if she did, and she could scarcely believe it when he provided the answer himself. 'You can't have got the rough edge of Juana's tongue this time because she's been at the practice ring all morning!'

'And you have to ask me——'

She turned on him, her eyes bright and angry but hurt too, then she got to her feet and hurried out on to the *patio*, seeking at least a pretence of privacy. Inevitably Eduardo followed, grabbing her arm the minute they were out of sight of the family in the *salón*, and spinning her round to face him. 'Lari, for God's sake!'

'Don't grab me!' she declared huskily, more angry because she was so close to tears and really the situation was nothing new. 'I can't really believe you're so—so insensitive as to think I wouldn't care that she spends the whole morning with you!'

'Not with me!' Eduardo denied, his dark eyes gleaming. 'Sitting with the organiser of the *fiesta*! I've spent the morning with two particularly nasty-tempered *novillos* and even managed to get myself nicked because I was thinking about my wife instead of what I was doing!'

Lari paled visibly and her hands fluttered to her face, gazing at him over her fingers and feeling sick suddenly. 'You—you didn't say anything,' she whispered, and he cut short any expression of her anxiety.

'It was a nick, nothing more, it barely drew blood, and I'm not in the habit of making a fuss about anything as slight as that. What concerns me more is to come home and find you almost literally turning your back on me.'

The scent of oranges and magnolias was head-spinning in the afternoon heat and there had been a stillness that their intrusive presence disturbed, so that a small bird fled from the bower of magnolias in noisy indignation and startled her. Eduardo still held one arm, but he eased his grip slowly and he was shaking his head, so that she knew he was going to try and explain to her.

'You are a little fool,' he said softly, and easily overcame her swift attempt to break away from him by tightening his fingers. 'No, *amada*, you shan't run away from me, you'll stay and listen to what I have to say!'

'I don't want to listen to your excuses, I've heard them all before!'

Tears brimmed into her eyes and she felt weak and oddly helpless as she stood facing him, yet not looking at him because she knew so well that it could be her undoing if she did. His voice did not suggest he was seeking to appease her, and she dared not look up and see if his eyes confirmed its harshness.

'I've never made excuses and I've no intention of making any now,' Eduardo informed her flatly, 'but you *will* listen to what I have to say because I say you shall!'

'Tell it to Juana Cortez!' Lari retorted huskily, tugging to free her arm. 'She's what you want, not me!'

'Stop it, do you hear me? Stop it!' He shook her so hard that her teeth rattled, then caught her to him suddenly and bound her close with his arms while he buried his face in her hair. He was breathing hard and the tumultuous violence of his passion thudded against her own anxious heartbeat like a drum. 'This is all because you saw me leaving with Juana this morning, isn't it?' He sounded much quieter now, and Lari nodded as best she could, having no desire to confirm it verbally. 'And you think I dissuaded you from coming because I'd arranged it with her beforehand?' Another nod confirmed it, and he sighed deeply. 'Oh, Lari, why are you so insistent that I'm having an affair with Juana?'

He sounded much more reproachful than angry now, and Lari ventured an upward glance, though it was far too difficult to meet his eyes. 'You—you did once,' she murmured. 'Marta told me that you and Juana were——'

'Marta?' He gave a deep sigh of exasperation. 'And I thought she liked me!'

'So she does,' Lari assured him unhesitatingly. 'She thinks I'm very lucky to be married to you.'

'But you don't agree with her?' Eduardo guessed, and Lari brushed an anxious tongue over her lips, thinking how lucky she had thought herself only hours ago.

'I—I don't know,' she whispered. 'I want to love you —I *do* love you, but——'

'You don't trust me!' he guessed drily, and Lari flinched from the truth of it. Taking both her hands, he led her to a seat set under an orange tree and sat them both down on it, still holding her hands. 'Lari—years ago, when I wasn't much older than you are now, I *did* have what you're pleased to call an affair with Juana. She is, and was then, a very sexy lady and I'm no more of a monk than most of my sex. But then she married Hugo Cortez and as far as I was concerned that was an end of it; I wasn't brokenhearted and I'm quite sure Juana wasn't. She's here because she's family, but now——'

'Now?' Lari prompted, and her eyes watched him anxiously.

'Now,' he echoed softly, 'I have an adorable young wife who loves me and whom I love very much, and that, in my estimation, puts Juana nowhere at all.'

'But that isn't what Juana wants or means to allow, Eduardo.' She did her best to make it sound matter-of-fact, but she knew even before she finished saying it that Eduardo wasn't going to accept it, even now. 'That's why she tried to cause me injury—or worse—when she moved that warning card on the store lift.'

'Lari!' The faint hint of exasperation in his voice flicked her like a whip and she shrank from it. 'This is becoming an obsession with you and it's got to stop! I know just how bitchy Juana can be and there's probably some truth in what you say about her not liking the fact that I married you, but—good God, girl, you can't seriously believe her capable of attempted murder, I won't believe it!'

They were right back to the beginning, Lari realised despairingly, and her eyes flooded with tears. 'I knew you wouldn't,' she accused throatily, and he gripped her hands more tightly than ever.

'How can I?' he appealed. 'I've known Juana for most of my life! how can I suddenly believe her guilty of trying to manoeuvre an accident in cold blood because she doesn't like my being married?'

'Women have done worse for love!' Lari insisted in a voice that shook with the sobs she was trying hard to subdue. 'I saw her there, Eduardo, you didn't! She meant me to be—be hurt; I—I dare not think she meant me to die, but I know she meant me harm, and until I can make you understand that and believe it, Eduardo, I can't—I *daren't* be a proper wife to you! I daren't!'

'Lari!'

She struggled free of him and stood for a second with tears streaming down her cheeks, her eyes blinded with them, then she caught her breath in a choking sob and turned to run back into the house. Heedless of how many eyes followed her erratic progress through the *salón*, she made for her room, and once there she flung herself down on the bed where only hours ago she had reached the peak of ecstasy in Eduardo's arms, and cried as if her heart would break.

CHAPTER SEVEN

THE two days following seemed endless to Lari, and she knew that if only Eduardo had come to her she would have given him her love as readily as she had on that first occasion, no matter if she had made a vow to the contrary. Instead she had lain through the long dark hours in solitary misery because he had taken her at her word, falling asleep in the early hours of the morning.

It might have been easier too if he had treated her more harshly or even ignored her altogether, but his manner was gentle and quiet, and betrayed no emotion whatever. That perhaps was the hardest of all to accept, because it made her fear that she might have driven him into the more than willing arms of Juana Cortez.

There was a great deal of bustle and excitement on the day of the *fiesta,* and the *corrida* was the subject most on everyone's lips. Eduardo had appeared many times in the local bullring, beginning as a *novillero* in his early twenties, and working up to a fully fledged *matador* with quite a following among the local experts. But Lari had never before been closely associated with that side of his life, and no matter how hard she tried to come to terms with it, it became no easier to accept. She certainly couldn't look forward to it with the same pleasure and excitement as his family did.

Nevertheless there were other things to enjoy and she had promised him she would be there to watch him, though whether or not he still wanted her to hold to it, she couldn't even guess. She had barely time to reach her bedroom to change and prepare for the big event when someone tapped lightly on her door and she turned swiftly. Her heart was beating hard and fast and she prayed it might be Eduardo, even while her common sense told it was not possible, and she was still trying to convince herself her common sense could be wrong when she heard voices outside her door.

Neither was a man's voice, and curiosity made her walk over and open the door instead of calling to whoever it was to come in. She found one of the maids there, young and obviously flustered, holding tightly to a large dress box which she appeared ready to guard with her life if necessary. Facing her and seemingly prepared to make her hand it over was Juana Cortez, her dark eyes bright and menacing, her dark red mouth set into that trap-like thinness that was all too familiar to Lari.

The moment Lari opened the door the girl bundled the box into her arms as if she could not wait to part with it, gasping out her message quickly and breathlessly. 'For you, *señora*!'

'For me?'

Her apparent doubt seemed to confirm Juana's suspicions, whatever they were, and she snapped harshly at the girl, despising her nervousness. 'You see, you fool, the *señora* isn't expecting anything to be delivered! Were you?' she demanded of Lari.

'No,' Lari admitted, still a little dazed by the suddenness of it all. 'But if Rosa says——'

'The girl's a fool!' Juana decided sharply.

'Where did it come from, Rosa?' Lari's quiet question was far more reassuring and the girl answered her unhesitatingly.

'It came yesterday, *señora*, and Señor Eduardo told me to bring it to you when you came up to change to go to the *fiesta* today.'

'Señor Eduardo?'

They were in unison at least in questioning the donor

of the dress box, and Juana looked more darkly suspicious than ever. Despite her nervousness there was something in the girl's eyes that brought a hint of colour to Lari's cheeks, but she knew without looking what Juana's reaction would have been to that. She knew too that the girl looked to her to support her in the face of Juana's anger, and Lari did her best.

'Tell me, Rosa, please.'

'I took in the package yesterday, *señora,* and Señor Eduardo himself told me to keep it until I saw you come up to change today and then to bring it to you; to the *señora,* his wife, he said, and I have done as he asked me to, *señora.*'

'And you've done as he said, Rosa, thank you.'

The look on Juana's face brought little chill shivers to Lari's skin, though she would not have admitted it for anything. Defeated but still not completely convinced apparently, Juana turned away, leaving a half-spoken threat in the air. 'If I find you've made a mistake, my girl——'

She went stalking off towards her own room while Lari and the little maid watched her go, and despite the half-made threat it was doubtful if the other girl was as chilled by Juana's anger as Lari was, even though she did her best to disguise it. 'Señor Eduardo isn't still here, is he, Rosa?' she asked, and the girl shook her head, relief bringing back her smile for a moment.

'No, *señora,* he left for the church about a half-hour ago.'

'Oh! Oh yes, of course.' The box she held bore the name of one of Seville's most exclusive dressmakers, and she was impatient to see what it contained. 'Thank you, Rosa.'

'*Señora.*'

When she had gone Lari carefully put the box down on the bed, contemplating it for a moment before she opened it, and her heart was hammering hard. There was a warm glow inside her that welcomed this gesture of Eduardo's just as surely as Juana Cortez resented it, and her hands were shaking a little as she lifted off the lid of the box.

Clouds of tissue paper impeded her for a moment, and then she was gazing at the sleek folds of deep yellow silk it had concealed. Her first reaction was to wonder that Eduardo could picture her in anything quite so exotic and just for a few seconds she had the uneasy thought that perhaps it had been meant for Juana after all. But the maid had been very insistent, and she knew her to be a bright and intelligent girl, not likely to have got the message wrong.

Lifting it out of its box, she held it against her, then after a moment or two put it on and regarded her reflection thoughtfully. The fact that it fitted her so perfectly was in itself sufficient to tell her there had been no mistake, for Juana Cortez was built on quite different lines.

Its fitted bodice moulded her shape cunningly and the neck was just low enough to allow a glimpse of bosom, the neckline bordered with a band of gold thread embroidery. Just below the fitted waist the skirt became more full, flattering her slender legs, and Lari realised as she twirled experimentally in front of the mirror that it was simply a less flamboyant adaptation of the Andalusian carnival dress.

Just the thought of Eduardo having had it made for her was thrill enough, but to realise that he must have understood how well it would suit her added to her pleasure. He had realised that she did not have the same bold flair as the native Andaluz for frills and flounces, but he evidently saw her as having maturity and warmth enough to wear that rich deep yellow without being overwhelmed by it, and that somehow did a great deal for her morale.

She would like Eduardo to have seen her in it before he went, and she felt hurt that he had not come to say something to her first; given her the opportunity to wish him well. Following custom he would have been without food for nearly eighteen hours by the time he appeared in the bullring, and she supposed the visit to church was another part of the preparation, but she would like to have seen him again first.

She stepped outside her room and turned to close the door, turning quickly when a sound further along the gallery caught her attention; her heart almost stopped beating when she saw Juana standing by the door of her own room and evidently making for the bathroom that adjoined it. Her tall slender figure was clothed in a silk robe and she took note of the yellow dress for a second or two before turning swiftly and reaching for a large pottery vase full of carnations that stood on a wall table beside her.

Some sixth sense warned Lari in the same moment, and when the vase and its contents came hurtling along the intervening length of gallery she was able to move in the nick of time, leaving the white-painted wall to take the full force of the missile. Scented heads of carnations tumbled to the floor along with shards of broken vase, while rivulets of discoloured water ran down the wall in yellow stains and on to the carpet.

Lari didn't wait to see the look she knew would be in those huge black eyes, but turned and hurried along to the staircase, caring only that her precious yellow dress had escaped being spoiled, and ignoring the sound of scornful laughter that followed her. But Juana Cortez, she felt, still had far too much of the upper hand, and she wished she could do something about it without further incurring Eduardo's wrath. She was dangerous, whether or not he recognised it.

Lari was much earlier than she need have been and there was no one else about when she came downstairs to the *salón*, but her mood was at variance with the festiveness of her dress. Not only had she the bitter hatred of Juana Cortez to contend with, but her fears for Eduardo as well, and she was looking as anxious as she felt when she turned quickly at the realisation that someone had followed her into the *salón*.

'Eduardo!'

His appearance was so unexpected that her pleasure at seeing him was completely undisguised. Her heart was thudding wildly and her instinct was to reach out to him; to get as close as it was physically possible and hold on to him tightly. Instead she stood just inside the *salón*, tinglingly aware of him while he took slow and explicit stock of her in the yellow silk dress.

'I'm glad you're wearing it,' he said, and she smiled.

'Oh, but of course I'm wearing it,' she told him, and made no pretence that it did not please her. 'It was such a wonderful surprise when Rosa gave it to me, and—and I wanted to see you before—to thank you.' Her smile did not quite reach her eyes, for seeing him seemed to increase her fears for him, and it was hard to disguise it. 'It fits me perfectly and the colour is gorgeous. I—I've never worn anything yellow before, but I can't think why; it suits me, doesn't it?'

She was talking simply to calm her anxiety and he knew it. But as well as the familiar air of gentleness, there was something else about him too that she noticed. A deeper and much more intense emotion glowed deep in his eyes when he looked at her, and started up those wild, dizzying desires that she found so hard to control.

'It suits you very well,' he agreed, and traced the low neckline with a forefinger. His touch made her shiver as it always did, and when it brushed lightly across the soft swell of her breasts it lingered for a moment before he reached for her hand. 'Will you talk with me until I have to go?' he asked, and Lari wondered if he seriously thought she would deny him.

'Yes, of course I will.'

He said nothing, but his long fingers tightened their hold as he led her out on to the *patio* and she realised that this was their first moment alone since that dramatic exchange two days before, in almost exactly the same spot. Somehow the air of intimacy, and the sense of peace in the gardens made her own inner turmoil seem more out of place than ever, and yet she couldn't shake it off, try as she might.

Under the scented orange trees his dark face had a shadowy mystery that emphasised sculpted cheekbones and black-fringed eyes, and she had never before seen him look so gravely austere. Nor had she ever loved him as much, or needed him more desperately than she did at that moment when they stood facing one another and holding hands.

His fingers had a subtly caressing touch, and when he reached out and stroked a hand slowly down her cheek, she turned her head and pressed her lips to his palm, half closing her eyes in the ecstasy of contact. Leaning forward, he lightly kissed her throat where a small pulse throbbed urgently, and lingered there until she lifted her face and yielded up her mouth to him.

'Lari!'

He whispered her name huskily, and drew her close to the vigorous warmth of him, his hands gently compelling, pressing her ever nearer until she made a soft little moaning sound and lifted her mouth eagerly, anxiously searching for the response she knew he was bound to make. He touched her lips lightly, and his breath was warm on her mouth, his voice harsh with the passion that burned in him and sought to touch her too.

'I couldn't go today without making up with you first! I don't know how I've stayed away from you, my love; I almost didn't, but I wouldn't—I *couldn't* bring myself to beg for something you weren't willing to give freely!'

'Oh, if only you had!' Lari whispered, seeking the more fierce touch of his mouth. 'If only you had, my love, you don't know how much I longed for you to come to me!'

He looked down at her with eyes that burned like jet between their thick lashes, and searched over her face slowly, as if to remind himself of every single feature of it. 'When this is over,' he promised softly, 'I swear I'll never go into the bullring again. Today will be my last *corrida*, my little one, I have sworn that for your sake, and I'll abide by it!'

'Thank God!' Lari breathed, her eyes closed. 'I couldn't bear to go through this again, ever!'

'But you'll come this last time, won't you?'

It was hard to appear to accept it as easily as he seemed to expect, but she nodded agreement. 'I'll come,' she promised, 'but I *am* very glad I don't have to make the same promise again!'

'Baby!'

His voice was teasing but not the look in his eyes, and she lifted her arms and put them around his neck, every nerve in her body responding to the fire and vigour of him. She was prepared to yield to the need that wanted her as fiercely as she wanted him and when he sought her mouth she surrendered it as eagerly as he took it, and lost herself in the passion only he could arouse in her.

It was like surfacing after too long under water when her hazy consciousness registered the click of high heels on the *patio* stones, and she came back to reality only very reluctantly. The figure that came around a full-blown magnolia at one corner of the *patio* was unmistakable, but the bright yellow dress was unexpected and for a moment Lari stared at it unbelievingly.

The look in Juana Cortez's eyes when she first caught

sight of them sent trickles of ice running along Lari's spine, and for a moment or two, while Eduardo was still unaware of her presence, Juana stood in that form-fitting and highly erotic dress, glaring her malevolence. In the past couple of days she had probably taken heart from the obvious coolness between Lari and Eduardo, and finding them together now must have come as quite a shock. The way she regarded Lari was in itself a threat, though there was little likelihood of Eduardo recognising it.

'Oh, so this is where you are!'

It was incredible to notice how quickly that malevolent expression changed to a smile when Eduardo turned towards her, though his swift frown could have done little to encourage her. Nor did he miss the bright yellow dress, but took explicit note of it while Juana enjoyed every moment of it.

'Two great minds,' she said softly, and laughed.

'Did you want to see me for some reason, Juana?' Eduardo asked her, and something in his voice must have warned her not to go too far, for she was noticeably quieter when she answered, though not deterred by any means.

'Rosa told me you'd come back to the house and I thought I'd better come and warn you that it's getting quite late,' she told him.

'Thank you, I know the time.'

She could surely not have been accustomed to such a curt and discouraging response, but Eduardo was probably much too preoccupied with other matters to notice the way her mouth tightened suddenly. Nevertheless he turned with an arm around Lari's waist and started back to the house, following Juana's slim, taut figure along the stone path.

'It's too early for the rest of us to go, isn't it?' Lari ventured as they walked into the house, and it was Juana who took her up, her mouth hard and bitter.

'You're a complete novice as far as the *corrida* is concerned, aren't you?' she said. 'Have you ever been to one before, Lari?'

Lari wanted only a few more moments alone with Eduardo and she wished the other woman would go and leave them alone, though she had little hope that she would. In the event it was Eduardo who answered her, though he did so without raising his voice, and apparently without feeling the need to criticise her obvious contempt.

'Lari neither likes nor understands it,' Eduardo told her, 'and she agreed to come today only to please me, didn't you, little one?' Having explained her position, Eduardo obviously saw no more need to follow it up, and he turned to Lari, taking her hands in his and holding them tightly. 'Madre knows how you feel about it, *querida*,' he told her gently, 'and she understands that if you feel you cannot watch any more you'll leave and come home.'

The idea of her formidable mother-in-law doing other than despise her for her squeamishness seemed unlikely, and Lari pulled a face. 'I can imagine that it's no more than she expects of a weak-kneed Englishwoman,' she guessed, and laughed a little shakily, but Eduardo it seemed was intent on denying it.

'Not at all! The fact that you've agreed to go, feeling as you do about it, has impressed Madre with your courage, and be sure that if the flesh should prove weaker than the spirit, she won't blame you.'

It was an entirely new slant on her mother-in-law, but Lari could hardly doubt it was true coming from such an unimpeachable source as her son. 'Then I'll try not to disgrace her or you,' she promised.

'*Amada*!' He kissed her lingeringly, but even while he kissed her Lari sensed the malice of Juana's black eyes. 'I must go,' he whispered. 'Pray for me, little one.'

He let her go very reluctantly, and quite clearly he

did not expect Juana's next move, for he blinked in surprise when, instead of allowing him to walk past her, she stepped in front of him and reached up to put her arms around his neck. Without using physical force to evade her, which he would be loath to do, Lari guessed, he could not avoid her kiss either, and she kissed him full on his mouth.

Looking up at him, her bold black eyes both challenged and taunted him. 'I'll pray for you too,' she murmured huskily.

Very deliberately, Eduardo reached and unclasped her hands from his neck, then he removed her arms from him and pushed her away before turning back to Lari. His eyes burned fiercely, but with what emotion it was hard to tell; in the event he said no word to reproach Juana, only turned his back on her.

'It must be your kiss I take with me, my love,' he said to Lari, and drew her once more into his arms.

She heard the swift intake of Juana's breath and vaguely registered the *salón* door closing, then Eduardo sought her mouth and kissed her long and hard. There was a hot damp feel to his skin and Lari was reminded of something her stepfather had once told her; that part of a bullfighter's skill is conquering his own fear.

As Lari watched him go she was shaking like a leaf, for it was suddenly even more evident just how vulnerable that lean hard body was. She wanted to call him back, to beg him not to go, but she knew he would find it as hard to forgive her that as any of his family would. So instead she let the tears roll unchecked down her cheeks and thanked heaven that after today it was never going to happen again.

Lari didn't want to watch, and yet it was so difficult not to, and her stomach churned sickeningly. Her face was pale and she knew it, but thanked heaven that so far no one seemed to have noticed and commented on it. They were all too intent on the age-old spectacle that was being played out in the ring; seeing only the ritual and the courage, and taking the blood, the cruelty and the danger as part of the ritual.

It had all been so picturesque at the beginning, even Lari had recognised that, when the opening procession majestically marched across the ring. She had even felt a flutter of pride when Eduardo in his glittering 'suit of lights' walked in the right-hand position among the three *matadores*, as senior *matador*. It was when she saw his tall lean elegance in gold-embroidered yellow silk that she realised why he had given her the dress she was wearing, for they were a matched pair.

Unfamiliar in the black hat with the traditional pigtail clipped to his dark hair, he had an arrogance that was breathtaking and thrilled her in spite of the horror she felt for what was to come. But from the moment the president gave the signal to begin she did not once look directly at anything going on in the ring.

Most of what followed she glimpsed in very occasional glances upward, for she kept her head as bowed as she could without making it obvious that she was hiding her face. It was only when those nearest to her murmured excitedly that she raised her head in time to see Eduardo, hat in hand, formally requesting the president's permission to kill. The request granted, he made a half-turn on his heel and flung his hat in a wide arc towards the seats where his family sat.

Lari knew nothing of the tradition of dedicating a bull in that way, and so she merely sat and watched as it came whirling towards her, but Juana Cortez, well versed in the traditions of the *corrida*, rose majestically to her full height and caught the hat with graceful ease, clasping it to her breast for a moment while she looked down into the ring with a gleam of triumph in her great black eyes.

Once more the murmur of voices expressed interest,

for none could fail to know that their favourite *matador* was married to an English girl, and no one could mistake Juana Cortez for anything but a Spaniard. It was a rash and over-bold gesture and one that could only have been inspired by the fury of jealousy.

'Juana!' Señora Sagrera was not only surprised, she was shocked and Lari had never before seen her regard Juana the way she did then. Her attention distracted from the spectacle in the ring for the moment, she turned to Lari and obviously found her sadly lacking in some way. 'Larissa,' she told her firmly, 'you should have caught it, it was meant for you! Mother of God, child, have you no more pride than to sit there and allow another woman to take your husband's dedication of the bull when it was meant for you?'

Confused and flustered and wise only after the event, Lari shook her head, seeing no way of remedying the mistake. Juana Cortez sat there with the hat held firmly in both hands and her black eyes gleamed with both malice and triumph; there was no way she was going to relinquish it now. 'I didn't realise what it was all about,' Lari whispered by way of explanation. 'I didn't know it was going to happen, *señora,* or I'd have tried to take it myself.'

For a while it looked very much as if Señora Sagrera was going to berate her for her ignorance as well as for her failure to respond to her husband's gallant gesture, but then after a moment or two she shook her head slowly. 'It seems you know nothing at all about the *corrida,*' she allowed, 'and Eduardo should have told you what to expect. No matter, child, you cannot be blamed for failing to understand something you know nothing about.'

It was such an unexpectedly lenient view coming from her sternly fierce mother-in-law that Lari scarcely believed it. 'I wish I had known,' she murmured ruefully. 'I don't want Eduardo to think I deliberately didn't accept it because of the way I feel about—I mean——'

'I know what you mean,' her mother-in-law informed her briskly, 'and I'm quite sure Eduardo isn't so foolish as to believe you did it deliberately.' For a moment the severe black gaze was fixed on Lari's flushed face and she bore the scrutiny with as much composure as she was able. 'My son is very much—in love with you,' she stated flatly, and the slight hesitation suggested that she found Eduardo's feeling for her slightly indelicate. 'It's a pity your marriage cannot be put on to a more satisfactory footing.'

It seemed to Lari to be neither the time nor the place to discuss her relationship with Eduardo, and yet it was the first time her mother-in-law had even come close to any kind of personal conversation with her and she did not want to appear unwilling. 'It—there's a chance things could—might be better, *señora*,' she told her hesitantly, aware of Juana Cortez listening to as much of the conversation as she could above the noise of the crowded bullring.

'I'm pleased to hear it,' Señora Sagrera said, and turned to Juana, holding out her hand as she did so. 'Give that to me, please,' she demanded, indicating the hat she held. 'It wasn't meant for you, as you know perfectly well, Juana, and you should have been more discreet than to behave as you did.'

Juana's dark eyes gleamed with resentment. 'I have it——'

'And you'll relinquish it at once to its rightful owner,' Señora Sagrera insisted.

She wasn't a woman anyone defied for very long, if at all, and Juana eventually handed over her prize, which her mother-in-law immediately pressed into Lari's hands. 'Now,' she said, apparently satisfied that the wrong had been righted, 'let us see the skill with which your husband performs the *faena* before he despatches that brute.'

The last act before the 'moment of truth', and the most dangerous, was already being enacted down there in the ring, and Eduardo was now entirely alone with the bloodied animal, and armed only with a naked sword and the small red *muleta.* He swept the scrap of red cloth around the right side of his body with the grace of a dancer and drew almost a thousand pounds of blindly angry bull towards him, while Lari felt her skin grow cold at the sight of the blood that had already been spilled.

The sight of the wounded animal sickened her, and she fought both nausea and fear when another perfectly executed *natural con derechazo* brought roars of approval from the watching crowd. Hooves thundered on the muffling sand, but in her mind Lari was again feeling the touch of warm dark flesh pressed to her cheek, and the thought of it being torn and bloodied to provide a public spectacle made her ill.

Standing erect with the *muleta* in both hands, daring the weakening but still dangerous animal to touch him, Eduardo again earned the roaring approval of the crowd. But to Lari those wicked horns came too close and it was suddenly more than she could bear. With one hand to her mouth she got to her feet, and she was as pale as death, uncaring whether or not anyone witnessed her weakness.

The whole wretched thing sickened her, but worst of all was being aware of the awful danger Eduardo was in of being ripped apart by those huge horns. The *corrida* held nothing of pride and excitement for her, and her stomach heaved at the hot stench of the bullring combined with her own sickening fear. She was aware vaguely of her mother-in-law's enquiry as she got up from her seat, but she shook her head and waved a hand to indicate her preference for her own company.

The only thing she regretted about leaving was that she had almost certainly given Juana Cortez cause for satisfaction, but she couldn't help that, her inclination at the moment was to get as far away as possible from the bullring. She heard the crowd roar again as she made her way to the exit, and she was shaking like a leaf, her forehead beaded with moisture.

It was incredibly quiet near the exits, and the man she approached about finding her a taxi looked at her curiously—partly, she realised suddenly, because she was still clutching Eduardo's hat to her. The man guessed who she was, she thought, and he would scarcely believe that the wife of El Sagrera would wish to leave while her husband was still putting on such a fine display.

'Will you call me a taxi, please?' she asked, and the man heaved expressive shoulders as he complied.

Then he noticed the hand she held pressed to her queasy stomach and made expressions of sympathy with his mobile features. 'Señora Sagrera?' Lari nodded, hoping to discourage any discussion of her husband's qualities as a bullfighter. 'Such a pity you've been taken ill when El Sagrera is performing so magnificently, *señora*, eh?'

Lari nodded and even attempted a faint smile, while she sought to explain without making too much of a reaction that few Spaniards would understand. 'I'm not actually ill, it's just that——'

She waved a vague hand by way of explanation, unable to find the requisite words, and the man's sharp dark eyes gleamed while he tapped a forefinger against his nose and beamed her a smile of understanding. 'Ah, but of course, *señora*!' He opened the door of the taxi and solicitously handed her in, smiling all the time. 'Some women become squeamish at such times;

it is to be expected, of course, *señora*!'

'You're very kind. Thank you.'

Lari gave him a rather uncertain smile, then sank back thankfully in the seat. The man was already giving the driver instructions, and as she was driven off, he was assuring her through the open window that he would inform El Sagrera himself that she had left for home.

It seemed that she was scarcely away from the bullring before she began to feel better, by the time she arrived back at the house Lari was no longer feeling sick; only that nagging, inescapable fear for Eduardo remained, and there was nothing she could do about that until he came home safely.

It being *fiesta* none of the staff were home, and the big house had a strangely deserted air when she walked into it, but she was nothing loath to keep her own company for a while in the circumstances. It was much more pleasant out on the patio, so she sat out there and attempted to read a book to try and keep her mind off what might be happening at the bullring, for Eduardo had another bull to kill before it was all over.

It was possibly the combination of a number of things that brought about the feeling she had of sheer exhaustion. The emotional upheaval before they left the house, combined with very little sleep in the last two nights and the traumatic spectacle at the bullring, made her so tired that she drifted off to sleep eventually and knew nothing more until she became aware of someone holding her hands very tightly, and saying her name over and over in a deep soft voice that was thrillingly familiar.

'Lari? Lari? Wake up, my love! Please, Lari!'

Fuzzy with sleep in the first few moments she only half opened her eyes and looked hazily into the dark face that hovered close, smiling now that he saw she was waking up, but still anxious. Reaching up, she stroked a hand down his cheek and turned her head from side to side to bring herself more quickly back to consciousness.

'You're back!' she whispered, and he leaned and kissed her firmly on her mouth.

'Of course I'm back, you silly little creature, didn't you *know* I'd be back?' He lifted her into his arms and held her close, kissing her sleepy warmth lightly and teasingly until she lifted her arms and put them around his neck. 'I was told you'd come home in a taxi, so I came straight here,' he went on, his voice muffled in her hair. 'The others have gone on to the *feria*, but I wanted to assure myself that you were all right.' He raised his head for a moment and looked down at her anxiously. 'You *are* all right, aren't you, Lari?'

'Perfectly—now.' She kissed his mouth, trying to make him understand. 'I just couldn't—I'm afraid I just couldn't stick it out to the end, darling, I was too —too squeamish and I was so terrified that poor brute would gore you.'

'Not that you thought I didn't deserve it, eh?' he challenged, and because she had felt as she did about it, Lari didn't deny it.

She kept her eyes downcast and looked at the small pulse beside his mouth while she spoke. 'I hate it, Eduardo, and I'll never feel any differently, but most of all I was afraid for you.'

'I know, my love!'

He kissed her, his mouth lightly teasing hers. 'And now you're missing all the fun of the *feria*,' she whispered. Leaning back in his arms suddenly, she looked up with a warm, lazy smile in her blue eyes. 'You should have gone with the others, Eduardo.'

'You think so?'

He knew the answer well enough, and Lari shook her head, smiling again. 'I'm glad you came home to me instead.'

'I would have forfeited my second bull if I'd known you were here all alone, my love,' he murmured, and gathered her closer still.

Lari desired nothing more than to reassure herself that the lean exciting body she loved so well was unharmed, and she slipped open the buttons on his shirt with her fingertips, sliding a hand inside to lightly touch the olive dark skin and wiry black hair, and she was trembling when she felt it flinch and flutter in response.

'I was frightened as much for myself as for you,' she whispered, 'because I know I couldn't go on living without you.'

He took her mouth with that mingling of gentleness and ruthlessness that was so irresistible, and it was some time before she was able to think clearly again about anything. Then, cradled in his arms, she looked up at him curiously when he asked about her flight from the bullring. 'What did you say to the man who found you a taxi?' he asked.

'I don't know.' She wrinkled her brow trying to remember what she had said. 'I think I told him I wasn't really ill, but I—oh, I don't know exactly. Why?'

Eduardo's eyes were gleaming darkly and something in his eyes made her regard him suspiciously. 'Well, somehow, my dearest love, you gave him an impression I know can't be true, and he's probably told others by now.' He kissed her, watching her with his gently mocking eyes. 'He congratulated me heartily, not only on being awarded the ears of both my bulls, but on my virility. Somehow, my little one, he got the idea that I'm to become a father!'

'Oh no!'

Lari was startled, but Eduardo was laughing and kissing her flushed cheeks, as if he found the whole thing very much to his liking. 'Does it matter?' he asked. 'It could so easily be true, my love, though not quite as soon as our friend obviously expects.' His eyes gleamed down at her darkly as he held her close. 'It very much depends on you, my love.'

Lari knew exactly what he was asking of her. That she forget about what Juana Cortez had tried to do and resume that wonderful affinity they had shared a few nights ago, and she did not think she could refuse him. Her face buried against his shoulder, she closed her eyes and determinedly shut out the memory of huge black eyes agleam with malice.

Of a vase thrown in fury to try and ruin the dress he had given her, and the vicious look when the hat he had meant for her had been handed over so reluctantly. Most of all and hardest to forget was the lingering sight of a small white scar running diagonally across a slender ankle, and she wondered if she dared have Eduardo's child while the malicious threat of Juana Cortez still haunted her.

Lifting her face, she offered him her mouth, but her voice was husky with anxiety as well as the passion only he could bring her to. 'Love me,' she begged, and yielded once more to the love that not even Juana Cortez could make her abandon.

CHAPTER EIGHT

LARI had never been very good at hiding her feelings, and she was so delighted at the prospect of soon going home to Anchoterrias that she couldn't disguise it, whether or not it was tactful in view of their having been given temporary accommodation at Santa Inés. It was an especially thrilling prospect now that she and Eduardo were really man and wife, for it would be very different from those first uneasy days after their marriage.

Her in-laws, she thought, understood and sympathised with her pleasure at going home, but not so Juana Cortez, for she had done little to conceal the fact that she didn't like the present state of affairs at all. It had suited her far better when Lari and Eduardo had occupied separate rooms, and she had no doubt revelled in the fact that they so often had not seen eye to eye on various matters. Having Eduardo under the same roof with her had suited her ideally, and even now she never missed an opportunity of dropping hints to Lari about what she claimed were his true feelings, so that consequently Lari avoided her as far as possible.

She couldn't fail to sense the other woman's hate, but now she was almost convinced that Juana probably never had been Eduardo's lover in the true sense, certainly not since his marriage, but her determination to win him over had become an obsession. She was also a stumbling block because Eduardo simply could not bring himself to believe she was as vindictive as Lari knew her to be.

At least her mother-in-law's attitude towards her

had changed for the better, and it was to Lari that she spoke, glancing up from her needlework briefly. 'You're looking forward to going back to Anchoterrias, Larissa?' she suggested, and Lari did not hesitate to agree.

'Very much so, *señora*! Not,' she hastened to add, 'that it hasn't been very pleasant staying here, and you've been very good to put up with us for so long, but I love Anchoterrias and I'll be very glad to go back.'

The younger son and his wife had already retired for the night, but the rest of them still sat talking in the *salón*, and it was nothing new for Señora Sagrera to take charge of the conversation. She did so now as she continued with her needlework, but steered the subject in the direction she required it to go.

'And of course your children must be born there.'

Taken completely by surprise, Lari coloured furiously, and resented the fact more than usual because she knew just how much Juana would appreciate her discomfiture. It was such an obvious probe, too, that Lari wondered if her mother-in-law could possibly have got hold of the rumour started by the man at the bull-ring the previous weekend.

She glanced across at Eduardo, but he was watching her with one of his small and oddly reassuring smiles that suggested he thought her quite capable of handling the situation herself. 'I sincerely hope so, *señora*,' she said, 'though it's a little too soon to anticipate yet.'

'Now that things have been put right between you, I hope it won't be too long,' her mother-in-law declared. 'Anchoterrias needs sons to carry it on, and I wouldn't like to think that my son had to leave it to a nephew as his uncle did.'

'He won't!'

Heaven knew why she sounded so sure, but her

confidence came from a need to defy a certain look in the older woman's eyes. Lari's own mother had failed to provide José Sagrera with the much wanted son, but since his first wife had also failed in that direction it was safe to assume that José himself had been at fault, although she would never have said so.

'You sound very sure!' Almost inevitably it was Juana who challenged her, and the look on her bold handsome features sent little chills fluttering over Lari's skin.

'I actually heard a rumour at the bullring on Sunday,' Señora Sagrera went on with deceptive vagueness. 'Apparently someone had got hold of the idea that the wife of El Sagrera was expecting a child—wishful thinking on the part of his devoted fans, no doubt.' Her shrewd dark eyes drew Lari's unwilling gaze in spite of herself, and held it steadily. 'I didn't deny it because it seemed the simplest thing to let pregnancy be thought the cause of your leaving the *corrida* so hastily, although of course I knew it couldn't be true; not so soon.'

It would also have served to save the pride of a proud woman, and dispensed with the need to admit to her daughter-in-law's squeamishness, Lari thought. 'Eduardo told me that someone had congratulated him,' she said. 'It must have been the little man who called a taxi for me. I felt so wretchedly sick that I had a hand on my tummy, but I didn't want to make too much fuss and I told the man I wasn't really ill. It's obvious that he jumped to the wrong conclusion.'

'And naturally no one would even think that the wife of El Sagrera was too weak-kneed to sit through even one of his fights!' Juana suggested.

It was the first time she had ever been quite so openly derisive in front of witnesses, and Lari wondered what effect it would have. She saw Eduardo from the corner of her eye start so say something, but in the event it was her mother-in-law who took command of the situation, qualifying her support with her customary brusque shrewdness.

'I rather think,' Señora Sagrera said, 'that Larissa's —reaction was more the fear of a women in love than because she found the *corrida* too much for her. Am I not right, child?'

It was kindly meant and Lari simply did not have the nerve or the discourtesy to explain that the whole sickening spectacle had been too much for her. Instead she nodded without raising her head, and spared only a brief glance at Eduardo, momentarily startled when she noticed his smile and the way one eyelid fluttered briefly in a suggestion of a wink.

'I was terrified of what might happen to Eduardo,' she agreed, and it was no more than the truth, just a little less, that was all. 'Anyway it's such a relief to know I'll never have to go through all that again.'

Her meaning was unmistakable, but the moment she said it it was obvious that so far Eduardo had told no one else of his intention to retire from the bullring. His parents exchanged glances, and Señora Sagrera's black brows showed a hint of frown, but she said nothing for the moment. Juana Cortez on the other hand looked so blazingly angry that it was clear to whom she attributed the decision.

'Eduardo, you can't give up, not now, not after Sunday!'

'The decision has already been made,' Eduardo informed her, but no amount of assurance would convince her that he had given up willingly.

'By whom?' she demanded.

Eduardo's frown should have quelled her, would have done in less emotional circumstances. 'I make my own decisions, Juana.'

'But why?'

Before he replied Eduardo sought and held Lari's

gaze, and she saw a certain regret for her impulsiveness in the look he gave her, but no blame. 'Why? Because I love my wife and I don't want her to go in constant fear of what might become of me if I continue with the *corrida,*' he said quietly. 'When she *is* eventually carrying our children I want there to be nothing to upset her and risk making her ill.' He glanced at his mother's dark inscrutable face, as if he sought her approval of his motives. 'Isn't that much more important than a few moments of glory?'

'I shall be sorry to see you retire from the *corrida,*' Señora Sagrera told him, 'but it makes sense in the circumstances, my son.'

'Only because he's married to an Englishwoman!' Juana's voice was harsh with emotion and she seemed not to either care or realise what sort of impression she was making. 'Why must you become less of a man just to please your wife, Eduardo?'

Colour showed below the darkness of his face, and his heavy-lidded eyes narrowed warningly, although it was clear that Juana was already regretting her rashness. There was a look of despair as well as defiance in her eyes as she sat taut and sullen in her chair. Eduardo's self-control had always been a source of wonder to Lari, and she found it no less so now, even though she suspected it was regret as much as anger that affected his reply.

'I shall feel no less a man fathering sons than I do facing bulls in the ring, Juana, and I shall derive considerably more pleasure from it!' He got up from his chair, tall and arrogantly confident as he held out a hand to Lari. 'Shall we go up now, my love?' he asked.

Heaven knew what would take place in the *salón* after they left it, but Lari had a feeling that Juana had suddenly outstayed her welcome. When she turned to close the door behind them it was irresistible to look across, and she met the unflinching hatred in those huge black eyes with a shiver of apprehension. Whatever changes occurred for the better, there was still the matter of Juana Cortez to be concluded. And Lari felt that the moment could not be delayed much longer.

Whatever had happened between the senior Sagreras and their guest after she and Eduardo left the *salón,* Lari would probably never know, but it seemed significant that Juana Cortez did not put in an appearance until just before the midday meal. She seemed composed enough outwardly, but that burning, resentful look still showed in her eyes, and during lunch she mentioned to Eduardo that she was returning to Casa Cortez the next day.

He looked momentarily surprised, then murmured something that Lari didn't catch, but from the way Señor and Señora Sagrera reacted it was fairly obvious that they already knew of the decision. Perhaps it had been suggested the night before, Lari thought, and could imagine that, much as she would have preferred a Spanish daughter-in-law for her eldest son, Señora Sagrera was not prepared to stand by and see his present marriage endangered.

'I hope you'll still give me the benefit of your advice, Eduardo,' Juana told him, and waited for several moments before he replied.

'You have a very efficient manager, Juana,' he told her quietly. 'I don't think there's very much I can do—if you're ever in desperate need, of course——'

A shrug completed the sentence, and Lari noticed the flush that coloured that bold confident face at such an obvious brush off. Incredible as it seemed, Lari almost felt sorry for her, for she had been so sure she could lure him away from such a young and inexperienced wife, and the past few days had shown her just how wrong she could be.

'Won't you be seeing Juana so often as you used to?' Lari asked when she and Eduardo walked out to his car after lunch, and he leaned back against the car door for a moment and regarded her in silence.

Reaching out, he cupped her face in his big hands and stroked the thumbs gently over her cheeks, his dark eyes unfathomable. 'Would you have minded if I did?' he challenged softly, and must surely have known the answer without her having to tell him.

Just the same she didn't admit it, for it would suggest that there was less trust between them than she hoped there was. 'I won't act like a jealous wife if she needs your help,' she promised. 'I trust you, my darling, even if I don't trust Juana.'

Her obvious and continued dislike troubled him, she had always known it, and he regarded her thoughtfully for a moment. 'I can understand how you feel,' he told her eventually. 'She's been a bitch to you, one way and the other, and it must have been hard at times not to—hit back.'

'She hates me.' Lari stated it as a fact, but she noticed the way he instinctively shook his head over it. 'She does, Eduardo, she always has, because of you.'

'Not hate, surely!' Obviously the suggestion of violence it conveyed made him uneasy, and yet he surely couldn't doubt the strength of Juana's feelings about either of them. 'You're two women who—can I say it without conceit?—want the same man, although until recently I didn't realise quite how strongly Juana felt, I have to admit. But hate? That's surely too strong a word, isn't it, my love?'

'You think so?'

Her own opinion was in no doubt and Eduardo would know what made her so sure, and he was frowning slightly while he studied her face with its downcast eyes. 'You're convinced of it because of that nonsense about Juana being responsible for what happened in that elevator, aren't you, Lari?' When she didn't reply, he sighed deeply, as if he resigned himself to never making her see sense. 'How can such a lovely little head harbour such devious ideas?' he demanded, then bent and kissed her mouth—such a hard, lingering kiss that it suggested a reprimand, and left her breathless. 'I swear, my darling, that you're the most stubborn little madam I've ever had to cope with, and nothing I say is going to make you change your mind about Juana trying to harm you, is it?'

Lari wished that just once they could talk about it without coming to the inevitable deadlock, for it was the one thing that still needed to be agreed upon between them. 'I—I know she was there,' she said, her voice low and husky because she feared so much making another barrier between them. 'You see her from the point of view of a—a member of your family, Eduardo, however distant, and you were—there was something between you once, wasn't there?'

'Once,' he agreed quietly. 'Before you were old enough to even know what that something was, my darling!'

'But it makes it harder for you to judge her—objectively,' Lari insisted. 'You weren't stuck in that awful elevator as I was–terrified out of my mind, and wondering if you were worried about me being rescued only because I could bring you Anchoterrias!'

'Lari!'

She regretted saying that, but it wasn't the moment to retract and she could almost feel Juana Cortez's malice rising up between them. 'Oh, darling, please don't pretend that you cared more for me than the estate, because I know it wasn't true!'

'*Wasn't* true,' he agreed, and Lari made a small, anxious and barely audible sound before turning her lips to the broad warm palm that caressed her cheek.

She closed her eyes and nestled her face against his

hand, seeking his response with the sensual frankness of a kitten seeking a caress. 'I wasn't blaming you,' she whispered, 'I know how much you'd always wanted Anchoterrias. But Juana Cortez is something we just can't see eye to eye on, and you'll never be able to understand how much she frightens me.'

'Still?' He seemed to find it so hard to believe. 'Oh, my darling little love, what a baby you are!' He kissed her lightly, but his eyes promised so much more, and his mouth was suddenly hard and passionate, betraying the deeper emotions that desired more of her than a kiss. 'Only two more days and I'll have you to myself,' he murmured, and again his mouth sought and demanded a response from her, so that she lifted her arms to hold his arrogant dark head down where it was. 'I have work to do, *querida*,' he breathed, all too soon it seemed, and gently disengaged her arms from his neck. 'I'll see you this evening.'

'I'll be here,' Lari whispered, then impulsively pressed a kiss to the firm line of his jaw as he turned to open the car door. 'I love you!'

There was a curious atmosphere at dinner that evening, and Lari thought of it as pregnant, for she got the impression that the whole group had an air of expectancy. She could think of nothing to account for it, and seemingly Señora Sagrera had at least come to terms with the imminent departure of her guest, for conversation was almost normal.

The customary cook was away for a few days and a woman from the village had been prevailed upon to take her place. She wasn't as good as the regular cook, but the meal was adequate and Señora Sagrera had even commented on the excellence of the sauce they had been served with their cod. It had come as a surprise to Lari to learn that Juana was apparently an excellent sauce chef, and had been trained in Seville to Cordon Bleu standard; the sauce, she admitted with a smile, was one she had prepared and cooked herself, and she had obviously enjoyed the ensuing compliments.

It was only when something became very obviously wrong that Lari began to suspect the reason for Juana's desire to make a last good impression on her relatives, and the suspicion grew apace with the cramping pains in her stomach. Perspiration beaded her forehead, as well as her upper lip, and her skin felt curiously chill.

She knew the signs and she would have left the *salón* as unobtrusively as possible, but inevitably Eduardo noticed and reached for her hand. Feeling it chill and moist, he frowned at the paleness of her face and got up out of his chair quickly. 'Lari?' He crouched beside her, holding tightly to her hand, obviously appalled by the pallor in her cheeks. 'Darling, what on earth is the matter?'

'I—I feel—ill.'

'Sick?' She nodded, and he placed a hand on her forehead, frowning when he found it so damp. There was an air of almost naïve pathos about the smile she tried to give him, and he turned quickly and called to his mother. 'Madre, I think we'd better call out Doctor Moreno!'

'I'll go!'

His brother got up at once when he saw how she looked, and Señora Sagrera hurried across, placing a smooth cool hand on her forehead. 'You do indeed look ill, child,' she decided with unaccustomed kindliness. 'We *must* have the doctor.' It could have come as no surprise to anyone when she took charge of the situation, although Eduardo was already doing as she suggested before she said it. 'Put her to bed, Eduardo, and keep her warm. Have you any idea what this could be?'

The question had been addressed to her son, but it

was Lari who answered. In a small, thin voice that trembled as much from fear as from weakness, because Juana Cortez's black eyes gleamed like polished jet and confirmed her worst suspicions. 'I—ate something,' Lari whispered. 'There must have been mushrooms——'

'But we had nothing with mushrooms,' Señora Sagrera insisted, frowning perplexedly. 'Maria knows how they upset you, and she wouldn't have——'

'*Maria* knows!' Eduardo reminded her grimly.

The pains in her stomach grew worse by the minute and Lari shook her head helplessly back and forth while he carried her. 'She—she knew,' she whispered, and Señora Sagrera caught her words, but misread their meaning.

'But of course she did! I told the woman myself when she took over from Maria, I remember now. This is sheer, criminal carelessness, and I shall see that it isn't repeated in other directions!'

'See her, find out—and sack her!'

Eduardo threw the angry words over his shoulder as he went out, and the *salón* door closed on a murmur of voices, but Lari knew that not one of them would ever dream of suspecting Juana Cortez. Which of them would think one of their own number capable of hating someone so much that she would deliberately administer something she knew to be poison to her? Not with the intention of killing her, Lari allowed that, but in the hope of making her horribly sick and causing her pain. The very thought of being the target of so much hate appalled her, and she clung tightly to Eduardo as he carried her upstairs.

It seemed almost as if he was afraid to let her out of his sight, for he put her to bed himself, then sat beside her, soothing back the hair from her clammy forehead, and vowing vengeance against the temporary cook whom he saw as responsible. 'That stupid woman! I'll see that she never forgets this as long as she lives!' His violent and passionate anger was in her defence, Lari knew, but it was misdirected, and she wished there was even a chance of putting him right. She was convulsed with another spasm of cramps and immediately his fury turned to gentleness as he did his best to give her ease. 'Oh, my poor darling, I feel so helpless!'

Lari couldn't lie still for very long because she was so sick, and the thought kept going round in her head that Juana Cortez was going to get away with this latest attack on her too. She had no doubt at all in her own mind who had been responsible, and it made her more anxious than ever to convince Eduardo. She clung to him between bouts of nausea, and tried her best to impress him with what she was saying, although even now she held very little hope of convincing him.

'Eduardo.' She raised her head and looked up at him, and he brushed back her hair with gentle fingers. 'You must listen to me; Juana knew about——'

'Oh no, Lari!' He hugged her close again, clasping her so tightly that she moaned because he hurt her. 'You can't—you *mustn't* think of that! The new woman must have forgotten about not putting mushrooms in anything for you, that's the only feasible explanation!'

'But they were in the sauce, don't you see?' She clutched her stomach in agony when another wave of nausea threatened, her voice scarcely more than a whisper. 'There—there weren't mushrooms with anything else—it—it had to be the sauce.'

He had to concede that, she realised, but he did so very reluctantly, and immediately suggested grounds for vindication. 'But if it was in the sauce, Juana didn't know about you being allergic to them,' he said.

'But she did—I told her—when she came—to——'

She broke off because nausea overtook her again, and before she had time to recover the doctor arrived.

Eduardo disappeared into the background somewhere, and it was Señora Sagrera who stood watch while she was examined, very thoroughly, by the family doctor. His diagnosis was what they expected, but not his decision to send her to hospital, and Lari tried to protest, looking round for Eduardo to support her.

'It's common sense, child,' Señora Sagrera told her, overriding any possible objection from her son. 'You'll be better cared for in hospital, and Eduardo can go with you, if that's what's worrying you.' She had obviously not let the grass grow under her feet either, for she came up with the same solution that Lari had, though she too offered the same extenuation as Eduardo. 'The possible source of the trouble puzzled us at first, but then it occurred to me that there might have been mushrooms in that very excellent sauce that we had with our cod. If only I'd thought of it at the time, this might have been prevented, but the mushrooms had been liquidised, and so weren't easily detectable. Juana, of course, had no idea of what the outcome would be.'

'She—she did!' Lari insisted in a hoarse whisper, and reached up for Eduardo's hand when he came up beside her.

'My dear child, what are you saying?' Señora Sagrera probably thought she had misheard, and the strong fingers that held hers squeezed in warning so that Lari merely shook her head wearily and didn't reply. 'A little delirious, I dare say,' her mother-in-law speculated. 'You'll be much safer in hospital, Larisa, and you'll have your husband to hold your hand, hmm?'

Her husband would hold her hand, but she despaired of him ever admitting her suspicion of Juana Cortez, Lari thought wretchedly, and at that moment she made up her mind that as soon as she was well again she was going to settle the question of Juana Cortez once and for all. She would have it out with her and make

Eduardo see her for what she was. At the moment she was simply glad that he was there to hold her hand.

The two days that followed were like a nightmare, and something that Lari preferred not to dwell on, for she had never in her life been so ill before. If Juana Cortez had hoped to make her suffer for having Eduardo's love she had succeeded. The third and fourth day she had been a little better, but on her fifth morning in hospital she woke feeling so much better that she managed to smile at the doctor who came to see her.

'Perhaps now,' the doctor observed with a wry smile, 'your husband will cease to haunt our corridors and get himself some sleep! You look very much better this morning, Señora Sagrera; how do you feel?'

'Very much better, thank you,' Lari assured him, and glanced beyond him to the door of the ward. 'Is Edua— is my husband here now?'

'Not yet, rather to our surprise,' the doctor teased her. 'But I've no doubt he'll be here very soon now and thankful to find you so much better, eh?'

She felt weak, but at least the awful stomach cramps seemed to have gone, and Lari was anxious to get things back to normal as soon as possible. For one thing she wanted to get back to Eduardo, and she sought the necessary information from the doctor. 'How soon can I go home?' she asked, while he checked her pulse.

He finished what he was doing, then smiled down at her knowingly. 'You can't wait to leave us, eh?' Lari said nothing, but gave him a faint smile and nodded her head. 'Well, you need another couple of days, Señora Sagrera, and then I think——'

'Two more days?'

It sounded like a lifetime to Lari, and her anxiety must seem out of all proportion, she realised. After a moment watching her face and apparently speculating on the reason for it, the doctor heaved his shoulders in a shrug. 'Very well, one more day. When your husband comes to see you today, you can tell him that he can take you home with him tomorrow, but only on condition that he takes very good care of you.'

'I'll tell him, and he will!'

Dark eyes appreciated the delicate beauty of her small pale face and bright excited eyes, and the doctor smiled. 'I'm sure he will,' he told her, and turned to go.

The nurse who was accompanying him on his round was about to close the door when Lari called out to her anxiously, 'What time is it, please, Sister?'

An understanding smile showed for a moment on the face below the white wimple and the Sister checked the time on her wristwatch. 'It's almost ten o'clock, *señora;* your husband will be here any minute now, don't worry.'

'Oh, I'm not worrying,' Lari assured her hastily, but as she settled back on the pillows to wait, she had never felt so impatient in her life.

She was still waiting nearly two hours later and her heart thudded anxiously when someone tapped lightly and then came into the room. Her face must have betrayed her disappointment, for the young Sister who brought in a huge bunch of carnations and roses shook her head by way of apology as she laid the flowers across her lap.

'There's a card, *señora,*' she said, and stood by patiently while Lari slipped it from its tiny envelope.

It reminded her for a moment of the time Eric Truman had sent her that bouquet of white carnations, but the handwriting in this case was Eduardo's and she frowned over the brief message he had written. '*I'm sorry, my dearest love, but I'll see you tomorrow. Eduardo.*'

Her eyes were misty when she looked up, and she told herself she was being quite idiotic about it, for hadn't the doctor teased her about Eduardo's devotion to her? But no matter how she tried she couldn't rid herself of the feeling that in some way Juana Cortez was behind his failure to visit her.

'How—how did they come?' she asked, and the Sister shook her head retrieving the flowers from the bed and sniffing their scent appreciatively.

'I didn't see them arrive, *señora,*' she said. 'But if you'd like me to——'

'No. No, it's perfectly all right—thank you.'

'I'll put them into water for you and bring them back,' the Sister assured her, anxious, Lari realised, because of her mood. 'Is there anything I can get you, *señora*?'

'No, thank you.' There was nothing the young Sister could get for her, for the only need she had at the moment was for Eduardo, and he wasn't coming. Lari only wished she knew why.

CHAPTER NINE

LARI had insisted on getting up and she was prepared to defy anyone who tried to keep her in the hospital bed a minute longer. She wanted to be ready to go when Eduardo arrived to see her, and she was quite sure he would come as he had said he would. After a night's sleep she was taking a slightly less emotional view of his absence the previous day and she could scarcely wait for him to come and take her home.

He must have had a very good reason, she told herself, or he would never have stayed away, not after spending so much time at the hospital while she was ill. Nevertheless, despite all her assurances to herself, she waited anxiously, and the moment he came into the little ward she moistened her lips anxiously, looking at him with wide uncertain eyes.

'Lari!' He came swiftly across when she got rather unsteadily to her feet, and took her in his arms, hugging her tightly to him. And she wasn't mistaken, she thought, her heart's beat taking on a more thudding heaviness suddenly; there was something about him that was different, a curiously withdrawn air that made her more apprehensive than she dared admit. 'I was told you could go home today,' he said as he sat her down again on the bed, 'but I didn't expect to find you dressed and waiting for me. You got your flowers, I see.'

Lari was shaking, and not simply from weakness. There was something, and she had to know what it was; she was not to be sidetracked by anything else. 'Eduardo, what is it?' she ventured in a small voice. 'I feel—I have a feeling there's something wrong and you're not telling me.'

'Darling!' He kissed her mouth gently, but with that promise of passion that stirred every nerve in her body to response. 'How would you like to go home to Anchoterrias?'

Lari gazed at him with anxious eyes. There *was* something, he had practically confirmed it by changing the subject, but whatever it was it would be easier to face at Anchoterrias, and she nodded eagerly. 'You know I'd love it,' she told him huskily. 'Can we?'

'Right now, if you're ready to leave.'

'I've been ready for hours,' Lari assured him, and he pulled her more closely into his arms and kissed her hard, pressing her to the familiar length of him as if he was afraid to let her go again.

'Then let's go home, my sweetheart,' he whispered.

There was a lump in her throat a short time afterwards when Lari looked up at the sun-warmed spread of Anchoterrias set above the valley road, and she thought how wildly excited she would have been if it had not been for whatever it was that Eduardo had on his mind. When they turned on to the approach road the familiar dust devil whirled up and followed them along the road to the house, reminding her of the day she had stood and watched Eduardo arrive. The day he had asked her, eventually, to marry him—she didn't think she could bear it if he was now about to tell her that he had, after all, decided to leave her for Juana Cortez; and he definitely had something on his mind.

Marta appeared under the overhang balcony well before the car stopped, and Lari smiled at her with as much brightness as she could muster. Her legs were still very weak after days in bed, and there was no suggestion of her walking, for Eduardo opened the car door, then lifted her into his arms and carried her into the house.

'Welcome home, *señor, señora*!' Marta's bright black eyes shimmered with tears as she followed them through into the *salón* pushing a trolley with coffee and pastries. 'It seems so long, *senora*!'

Eduardo set her down carefully on to the huge high-backed settee, then sat down beside her, and Lari felt herself trembling. He was so grave-faced, and somehow Lari got the feeling that whatever it was he had on his mind Marta knew what it was, for she did not even stay to pour them a first cup of coffee, but discreetly withdrew.

'Shall I pour our coffee?' Eduardo asked, but Lari shook her head. Whatever it was she had to hear sooner or later, she wanted to get it over and done with now.

'Tell me first,' she said, and when he looked about to deny there was anything to tell, she shook her head urgently. 'I know there's something on your mind,' she told him, 'and—and if it's something I'm not going to like I'd rather hear it first and get it over with, Eduardo.' His silence seemed somehow ominous and her hands were so unsteady that she clasped them tightly together, her voice anxious as she looked up at him. 'Eduardo?'

He reached out for her suddenly and drew her close into his arms once more, and when he kissed her his mouth was hard and forceful. But for some reason she could not define, Lari got the feeling that it was a force that stemmed from desperation rather than passion and again her heart lurched sickeningly. Still she clung to him as if she feared he might at any moment go and leave her.

After a while she raised her head and looked at him, noticing the shadows that smeared darkly under his eyes, and a kind of gauntness in his lean cheeks that made him look much older than he ever had before. Filled with a heady mingling of emotions that included an infinite tenderness for his seeming unhappiness, she stroked a hand down one lean brown cheek, then kissed him lightly on his mouth.

'Tell me what's troubling you, my darling,' she whispered. 'You look so—so worried, and it can't be because of me, because I'm perfectly fit again now.'

'You could have died!' He held her breathtakingly tight and buried his face in her thick silky hair, and Lari began to realise what it could be that seemed to be troubling him so much. 'I could have lost you for ever!' His voice was muffled, but there was an unmistakable note of anguish in it that affected her deeply. 'And I would have had to live with the knowledge that I was at least in part to blame!'

'Oh, my darling, no!' She raised her head and stroked her fingers down his cheek, but Eduardo took her hand and kissed its palm with a fervour that made her shiver. She had been afraid his preoccupation concerned Juana, but now she began to wonder if he had at last begun to realise how right she had been about his former girl-friend, and she looked up at him enquiringly. 'Darling?'

He seemed to be having such difficulty saying what he had to say, and she wanted so much to help him if she could. 'Lari—my love; I didn't come to see you yesterday because—I was with Juana.' Lari felt sure that her heart actually stopped beating for several seconds, then resumed its pulsing with a heavy, deafening thud that seemed to fill her head. 'I—I couldn't leave her, my own darling, will you believe that?'

Too dazed to think, Lari moistened her dry lips. 'I—don't know.'

She eased away from him slightly, and tried to account for the curiously haunted look he had, a look she did not begin to understand. He curved a big hand around her cheek and there was nothing she could do but respond to his touch as she always did, whatever happened, his thumb stroking across her lower lip.

'She took her car out yesterday morning fairly early, to drive into Seville on a shopping expedition,' he went on in a voice that she realised was not quite steady, 'and she crashed just this side of town; at the road junction. She asked to see me, my darling, and I—I couldn't refuse.'

'No, of course you couldn't.' Lari's tongue again moistened lips that seemed horribly parched suddenly. 'I understand, Eduardo.'

'My love!' He leaned forward to kiss her mouth. 'I knew you'd understand. I stayed with her until she died, just after ten last night.'

It wasn't what she expected, and Lari's breath caught audibly in her throat. Juana Cortez had seemed so strong and indestructible and it wasn't yet possible to believe she was no longer alive. Juana had hated her, as Lari knew to her cost, but she had also loved Eduardo and that had given them one thing in common; for that reason Lari could sympathise with her.

She had once been in a position to marry Eduardo, if Marta's version was true, but she had rejected him in favour of a man with wealth enough to give her all the things she wanted, and ever since it seemed she had been trying to win him back. Now she had lost not only Eduardo but her life too, and Lari could not help but speculate on whether there might not be a connection there somewhere, however tenuous.

'I'm—sorry,' was all she could find to say, and she thought Eduardo would not expect her to express anything more.

He held her tightly, and that haunted look in his eyes was explained at last, she thought. 'She talked to me even before the priest saw her,' he went on, and again Lari's heart lurched in anticipation. 'God help me, Lari, I found it hard to forgive her even though she was dying!'

'But you did?' She asked it anxiously, for Juana had been close to him she knew. He nodded. 'She—she told you?'

Again he nodded, but he no longer looked directly at her and Lari wished he would, for she did not hold him to blame for failing to understand Juana's almost psychopathic jealousy. Then he looked up suddenly and held her misty gaze for a long time. 'Will you find it as hard to forgive me for being so—so blind, my love?' he asked huskily. 'I was so nearly responsible for what happened to you; I should have realised how Juana hated you; how deep it went, and I didn't.'

Her eyes bright with a tangle of emotions, Lari shook her head, 'I never blamed you,' she whispered. 'I love you, but I was never quite sure how deep your feeling was for me, and Juana was—had been very close to you, and she was very—very potent.'

'Oh, my sweet love!' He hugged her close to him, so hard she could scarcely breathe, whispering against her ear. 'When I think how easily I could have lost you! Juana *did* take down that warning card on the elevator, just as you said; she knew you by sight even though you didn't know her, and she knew you hadn't seen any more than her feet and legs, you couldn't identify her afterwards. She told me she acted on the spur of the moment–Holy Mother, she must have been out of her mind to even think of such a thing!'

'She loved you and you were set on marrying me,' Lari murmured. It was so much easier to look at it objectively now that Juana was no longer a continuing threat. 'And I don't think she meant to do anything more than frighten me badly, either time.'

He eased her away from him just a fraction, so that he could look down into her small pale face. 'She could have killed you,' he said. 'Twice she gambled with your life, my darling, and I found that very hard to forgive; even now in my heart, I'm not sure I have forgiven her, even though, like you, I don't think she meant to—to kill you.'

'Oh, but you must forgive her now, my love!'

'Do you?' he asked softly, and Lari rested her forehead against his and clasped both arms around him tightly.

'I have to,' she told him. 'She'd known you for years and she made a mistake when she married Cortez instead of you. It isn't easy for someone like Juana to admit they've been wrong, and when she realised that you and I were going to be happy together——' She shook her head, her heart genuinely in sympathy with Juana Cortez for the first time. 'I can't imagine anything worse than loving you and not being able to have you, my darling; now she's gone I can feel sorry for her.'

Eduardo sought her mouth again, gentle at first, then fiercely passionate like the big gentle hands that caressed her, coaxing and soothing, bringing her ever closer to the vigorous strength of his body. 'I shall never take a chance with your life again,' he whispered fiercely against her mouth, 'you're too vulnerable, my sweet love! Tío José must have known that you needed someone much older to care for you when he willed you to me with his estate, but I almost let him down!'

Lari looked up at him through heavy lashes, her eyes darkly glowing, as she sought to press even closer to him. 'Is that how you saw me?' she demanded. 'As part of the estate?'

'I know now that you're the most precious part of my inheritance, my sweetheart, and I think Tío José knew you would be, knowing us both so well.' He got up suddenly and glanced at the tray with its coffee cups and plate of sticky little pastries. 'Do you want coffee?' he asked in a lower, softer voice, and Lari looked up into his dark eyes and read his meaning perfectly.

'Not really.'

He half-smiled, then lifted her into his arms again, kissing her hard when she put her arms around his neck and brought his head down to her. His eyes were half closed as he looked at her and the promises they made brought a swift urgent beat to her heart as he held her close, one big hand curved caressingly over her breast.

'Then I think it's time you were put to bed,' he told her, and his voice shivered along her spine, deep and seductive. 'You're not strong enough to do too much yet, and the doctor said I was to care for you very carefully for the next few days.

Lari smiled, laying her head in the hollow between his chin and the strong column of his throat and turning her mouth to the warm brown skin that pulsed more urgently than normal. The newly painted walls gleamed whitely as he carried her upstairs and along the gallery, but she barely noticed how smart and new it all looked at the moment.

At the door of the master bedroom, the room he had occupied alone before they left for Santa Inés, he came to a halt and reached down to open the door. Lari looked up, her arms tight around his neck, her whole being tingling with the nearness of him and the excitement he aroused in her.

'The master bedroom?' she queried in a throatily husky voice, and her eyes teased him.

'The *master's* bedroom,' Eduardo corrected her firmly. 'Where else would you have me bring you, my love?'

He closed the door behind him with a well placed foot and strode across with her to the huge old-fashioned bed that had slept generations of Sagreras. He laid her down with infinite care, then sat beside her, looking down at her in silence for several seconds before he began to unfasten the neck of her dress.

'You must rest,' he told her softly. 'I want you well again, my love, and——'

'I'm not ill now,' Lari interrupted, and arched her body to let him slide the top of her dress off her shoulders, reaching up her arms and drawing herself up with them round his neck. 'Eduardo?'

He neither moved nor spoke for a moment, but Lari could feel the tremendous vigour of his body close to her own and her whole being longed for him as she had so often done in the past. He gently unclasped her hands from his neck and laid her back on the pillows and she noticed how his hands trembled, then he leaned over her and for a second or two his breath, warm and slightly uneven, mingled with hers.

He touched her mouth lightly and she made a soft little sound, closing her eyes when he buried his mouth deep in the welcoming warmth of hers, and she reached up and clasped her hands across his broad back. Her head was spinning and her body shivered in response to the light evocative caresses that brought a quivering glow to her skin, and when he muffled his face in the mass of her bright hair and kissed her neck and her smooth naked shoulders, her dazed eyes registered the familiarity of Anchoterrias for a second.

Turning her head, she sought that hard, demanding mouth again, so blissfully contented she almost purred. 'Welcome home,' she murmured in the few seconds she had to draw breath. 'Welcome home, my darling!'